GETTING DOWN TO BUSINESS
COPYRIGHT © 2013, 2019 by Ginger Ring

Photographer: Wander Aguiar Photography

Models: Jonny James and Amanda J.

Publishing History: First Scarlet Rose Edition, October 2013 Digital ISBN 978-1-62830-053-6

Printed in the USA.

Cover Design and Interior Format

Getting Down to BUSINESS

GINGER RING

THANK YOU FOR PURCHASING GETTING Down to Business. This was the first book I ever published and a lot of readers wanted more of this short story. When I received the rights back to it this year, I decided to add to it. I hope you enjoy this fun and sexy read.

PROLOGUE

~ JESSIE ~

"JESSIE, GET THE HELL IN here and for Christ's sake put some damn clothes on." Travis, her annoying brother, yelled from inside Sparky's garage, the business named after their father.

"I'm just taking the garbage out." Jessie Knutson rolled her eyes and strutted across the hot concrete toward the dumpster. Boys were such jerks. Only a few more days and she'd be out of this place. There was more to this world than being stuck working in a sweltering, grungy old garage every day. There had to be.

Jessie took her time and swung her hips, the small bag of trash thrown over her shoulder like she was going for a stroll. Travis was a pain in the ass. *'Put some clothes on'?* What was he complaining about? She was fully clothed. Who did he think he was anyway? Her father?

Nearing the trash bin, she tossed the bag on the ground and wiped the back of her hand across her forehead. Dang, it had to be over a hundred degrees today. West Virginia was stifling in the summer but the past week had been especially humid.

Lifting her tank top a little, she let the slight breeze cool her damp skin. Bending at the waist, she gathered her hair and redid her ponytail higher on her head. Sweat dotted the back of her neck. Having thick red hair was a burden sometimes, especially on a day as boiling as this one.

What she wouldn't give to be wearing a pair of flipflops instead of cowboy boots but her dad insisted they all have sensible shoes on their feet whenever they were in the garage and he was right. Her foot throbbed just thinking about the time Travis dropped a heavy wrench on her toe. Heck, she still flinched when the sound of a tool hitting the cement floor echoed in the bays.

Jessie arched her back and took a deep breath. Travis would return to college soon and she'd be starting business school as well. It hurt to think about leaving her dad and everything she knew behind but truth be told, she couldn't wait to get out of this place. Could. Not. Wait.

Sighing she bent over to pick up the bag and tossed it in the dumpster. Ben, her youngest brother, would have to pick up the slack when they left home but he didn't seem to mind.

Something hit the ground behind her and Jessie turned her head. A lanky teenage boy jumped out of a truck to pick up a pair of sunglasses. He hurried back inside and slammed the door. She met his gaze briefly before he ducked under the dashboard. Kids. Jessie shook her head, tossed the bag in the dumpster, and strolled back to the garage.

Travis stood in the doorway. His fists at his hips.

"See?" He waved his hand in the air. "See what you just did?

"What is your problem?" Jessie groaned. "Didn't I put the garbage in the right way?" She rolled her eyes.

"I'm not talking about that. What you just did to that poor boy?"

"Huh?" Jessie shook her head. "What are you talking about?" She leaned up against the car Ben was changing a tire on. At least her youngest brother was nice and quiet.

"I'm talking about the kid out there." Travis pointed toward the pickup truck parked outside. The name of the man that owned it escaped her but he was in talking to her father about some parts. That she did know, but what was up Travis' ass was beyond her. The guy needed to get a girl-friend and mellow out.

Again, Jessie shrugged and shook her head. "What?"

"He was hanging so far out the window staring at you, he nearly fell on his head. You," this time he pointed his finger in her direction, "are a hazard to mankind."

"Oh my god! A what?" She shoved him aside to go get a pop from the fridge. Root beer was her favorite and her dad made sure to keep it on hand. Pulling one out, she twisted the top off, and took a long, much needed sip. The cool liquid fizzled as it went down her throat but it, unfortunately, did nothing to remove her pain in the backside brother from her sight. This time when she faced him, he stood feet wide and arms across his chest.

"You heard what I said. You're just like our mother," he spat. Jessie's hand shook as she set the pop bottle on the nearby work bench.

"Travis, let it go." Ben wiped his hands on his shirt and glanced back and forth between the two.

"Oh yeah, you mean the woman that gave up everything to stay here in this dirt water small town and raise her kids?"

"I mean the one that was never satisfied with what she had and was a shameless flirt." Travis gritted his teeth.

Jesse lunged and shoved him against the car. Theirs was a love–hate relationship, that was for sure. She loved to despise him but would fight to the death anyone that meant to do him harm. She knew Travis would return the favor. Growing up, they'd roughhouse for hours but that had calmed as they grew older. Not so today.

Ben stepped up to hold Jessie back from punching her older brother's lights out but that didn't stop her from screaming every swear word she could think of.

"What the Sam Hell is going on out here?" Their father came out of his office, his face a bright shade of red. "You two cut it out right now before I take both of you over my knee, and don't think I'm kidding."

Travis mumbled 'yes, sir' and marched over to the other side of the room. Jessie and Ben just nodded and stood where they were.

"Sorry, Spence. These kids will be the death of me yet." Her father exhaled with a huff.

Jessie frowned. Her father had a business meeting and they were acting like wild animals. "I'm sorry. We didn't mean to disturb you."

"You didn't, dear." The man, or Spence, as her father addressed him, just grinned and shook hands with her dad. "I got my own pack of wolves at home and I better get going before the one in the truck gets into trouble. Thanks Sparky. I'll be in touch." He nodded and walked outside to his vehicle. Everyone in the garage remained where they were until the sound of the truck going down the road couldn't be heard.

"Is someone going to tell me what that was about?" Her dad glanced from kid to kid.

Travis tossed a rag on the counter and turned around. "Yeah, she needs to dress more appropriate."

Jessie's mouth dropped open. "Are you kidding me?"

"As much as I'd like your sister to dress like a nun, that isn't going to happen. She's in a tank top and shorts just like every other girl her age. If she wasn't your sister, would you have a problem with it?" Her father was always the voice of reason.

"Well, no but not everyone looks like her." Travis glanced her way and shook his head. "What if someone tries to take advantage of her? I see the way men look at her and we're not going to be around to protect her." Her brother's concern softened her anger, but just a little bit.

"We can't keep her tied down here. Everyone deserves the chance to test their wings, even though it will hurt to see them go." Sparky sighed. "You mother was the same way. A thirst for adventure and zest for life. I miss her every day."

Her father's words touched her heart. It was all her mother ever talked about. Traveling the world and seeing exciting places but she never got the chance. Jesse bit her lower lip. A bout with a fast-growing cancer ended any chance of that.

After their mother died, her dad made it a point to include everyone in the decision making for the family. It'd been an adjustment when Travis left for school and it was going to be even harder for those left behind when she was gone as well.

"Jessie has a smart head on her shoulders. Her mother and I raised her well."

Jessie's thoughts returned to the present when her dad spoke up.

"Just like we worry about you, Travis, we will worry about Jessie and there's not a damn thing we can do about it when each other isn't in sight. I just hope and pray that all my kids are safe and sound." He pulled her brothers and her together in a group hug. "I'm proud of you all."

A lump formed in her throat. In a few weeks she'd be starting college in Ohio. She'd miss this place and even her jackass brother, Travis, but it wouldn't be home anymore. There was a whole world out there just waiting for her to discover. Never would she stay in one place too long. Never would she give up everything for some small-town boy. Never would she let someone else tie her down.

Her mother didn't get the chance to live out her dreams, but Jessie was determined to do it all.

CHAPTER ONE

~ JESSIE ~

15 years later, Blue Valley, West Virginia

"YOU NO GOOD PIECE OF crap." Hands on her hips, Jessie struck the flat tire with the toe of her black leather pump. She'd kicked it twice already in the last ten minutes, the first time due to frustration, the second time in retaliation for scuffing her favorite pair of shoes. Exhaling, she tucked a flyaway section of hair behind her ear.

The day couldn't get any worse. She'd lost a button off her blouse, ripped her skirt, and now on the hottest day of the year, she stood alone on the side of the road because of a bum wheel. Checking her cell phone once more for service, she cursed the surrounding West Virginia mountains before tossing her useless phone back in the car.

Weighing her options, she gazed back in the direction she'd come from. A long walk back into town held no appeal. Ironically, she'd been heading toward Spencer's Auto Repair just down the road, she wasn't sure how far it was or whether it was still open. As a representative and salesperson for

Bauer Auto Supplies, this was her last stop of the day.

Jessie had called earlier and left a message on their machine stating she probably wouldn't make their appointment due to the severe thunderstorms in the area that had given her a slow start. She'd made surprisingly good time and, not wanting to miss out on a new account, she decided to try to make it there before they closed.

"Damn that flat tire." Jessie kicked the tire one last time. Having grown up around cars, she knew how to change a flat. She just wasn't in the mood to change one wearing a skirt and high heels. Glancing at her watch, she folded her arms across her chest and tapped her toe. She'd give it another ten minutes before digging a pair of jeans and boots out of her overnight bag. The rumble of thunder in the background made her hair stand on end, literally, and she shortened the time to five minutes.

Leaning up against the door of her red coupe, Jessie took in her surroundings. It had been months since she'd been in her home state of West Virginia. The joyful song of wood warblers drifted from the trees. The fragrance of native wild onions floated in the air. She loved the hills, the lush forests, and friendly people. Despite spending years yearning to see the world, the constant travel of her sales job was wearing on her. Sure, she had an apartment in nearby Charleston, but she was never home.

The sound of a vehicle coming down the road brought Jessie's thoughts back to the present. Her pulse raced. She grabbed her purse so it was in easy reach, the calming weight of her small handgun tucked inside returned her heartbeat to normal. Fortunately, she'd never had to use the thing, but it was a comfort to have it with her in some of the areas she visited.

Her hands started to sweat. She crossed her fingers that the advancing vehicle included a knight in shining armor, and not a serial killer on the loose looking for saleswomen with flat tires. With the site of a wrecker coming toward her, she breathed a sigh of relief. The truck braked, coming to a stop on the opposite side of the road.

The driver's side window rolled down and a handsome face poked out. "Afternoon, ma'am. Do you need some help with your car?" He had dark hair, smoky eyes, and sexy stubble. Hell, the man was drop dead gorgeous if she did say so herself.

Finally finding her voice, she answered, "I'm so glad to see you. I've got a flat. I can't get any bars on my cell out here, and I really didn't want to have to change my tire in a skirt." She plucked at the hem with her fingers as he stared down at her with those striking dark eyes. Everything Jessie said was true but she still felt foolish rambling on. Blushing, she kicked an imaginary stone with her foot before resting her hands on her hips.

He cocked his head when he heard her answer. She was used to it. Having such a low, raspy voice she was often mistaken for a man on the phone. That worked to her advantage as garage owners were more likely to make an appointment with someone, they thought was a guy and it knocked them off guard when they found out she wasn't.

"Well, let me take a look and see what we can do." The wrecker driver grinned and turned off the engine.

His low, rich voice had a slight Southern drawl. To hell with the car, she wanted him to do some service work on her. Just the sound of it made her panties melt. What a girl wouldn't give to have him whisper sweet nothings in her ear while feeling the breeze of his breath on her neck! Jessie's heart skipped a beat and her knees weakened.

The truck door squeaked open. He eased out of the wrecker with the grace of a dancer. His work boots sounded on the hard pavement as he advanced in her direction. Jessie bit her lip as she did a quick scan of the rest of him. The man was tall and lean with a certain swagger to his step. He wore blue denim jeans slightly worn at the knees and what looked to be black motorcycle boots. Did he have a bike?

If he did, his score on the hotness meter just went off the charts. His light blue work shirt, unbuttoned and hanging loose, showcased a slightly hairy chest and six pack abs. Yummy. The initials BJ embroidered on the pocket sent another line of erotic pictures floating across her thoughts.

A slight glistening from the humid air gleamed on tan, muscular forearms dusted with black hair. Flashes of black ink decorated his skin. Her heart rate accelerated as she stared into eyes that matched the darkness of onyx. Approaching the flat tire, he caressed the rim around the cause of her distress, his strong hands slightly stained with work.

She remained quiet. Her eyes followed as he straightened and circled her vehicle. His hand never left the smooth, warm surface of the car as he surveyed it for other ailments. Jessie's sensations were on overload as she imagined those gentle fingers gliding across her curves. Rounding the front of her vehicle, the man gave her a smile and a shy onceover of her body before turning his attention back to the tire. Was the slight pink on his cheeks a blush or from the heat?

Jessie turned, hoping to hide the smirk. Men, they were all alike. Did he like what he saw? She would be a fool to think her long legs and C-cup breasts hadn't added to her sales somewhere along the way. She knew her best assets and wasn't afraid to use them, but in this case, she wanted him to find her attractive, not want to buy something from her.

The whole thing was odd. She wracked her brain trying to remember the last time a man lit a spark in her. Yet, here they were on the side of the road and all she could think about was him. Who was he? Was he married? Girlfriend? God, she hoped the answer to both those questions was a big fat no.

BJ prowled like a panther as he approached her, his hand still touching the warm metal of her car. He looked even better close up. Dark, wavy hair touched the back of his neck, damp from the heat of the day. His face tan from the sun, his deep brown eyes still locked on hers. High cheekbones graced his chiseled face, while a day or two's worth of whiskers accented his jaw. How she wanted to feel his rough jawline along the smooth skin of her inner thigh. Okay, now this was just weird. She took a deep breath. Maybe her hormones were just out of whack?

Her eyelids dipped as they settled on his sweet lips. Despite the heat, her nipples hardened. A flash of sunlight reflected off a buckle on his boot and her gaze dropped to his feet. She'd always loved men with long legs. Those tight blue jeans showed off his muscular thighs to perfection.

Jessie hated to admit it, but she'd been too long without a man. That had to be the only logical reason for her reaction. The only action her lower half had seen in the last six months belonged to a battery-operated toy packed in her suitcase. She'd never been into one-night stands but traveling left little time for dating.

This man was at least six feet tall, maybe even six two. By the looks of his big boots, he was sure to have the right equipment to make her engine purr. What should she do? His left hand was wedding-ring free. Would he be interested in her? He looked a couple years younger, did he like older women?

She licked her parched lips. Her eyes followed a bead of sweat trailing down his throat into the nest of dark, curly chest hair. It worked its way south through a forest of curls, and along the hills and valleys of his abs. She felt lightheaded from the heat of the day and the intensity of his gaze. Her mind flashed to what the rest of him might look like. The parts covered up by clothes.

Her body temperature rose. She brushed the back of her hand across her feverish forehead and closed her eyes. Jessie tried to swallow, her throat suddenly parched, too. Was it from the heat of the day or the hotness of her rescuer? Her hands trembled and her head swam in confusion. Drooling over a stranger was so out of character for her. She was always the ice queen. Nothing could thaw her heart. Just make the sale and hit the road.

"Are you all right? You look a little pale." BJ grabbed her elbow, guiding her toward the driver's side of his truck. He swung the door open, reached across the seat and grabbed a bottle of water from a white cooler occupying the passenger seat.

As she stood in front of the door, the coolness of the cab refreshed her immediately. The sips of cold water invigorated her also but being so close to such a fine-looking man was definitely making her thirsty for other things.

"Climb in and cool off. It has to be over a hundred today. When you're up to it, we'll head back to the shop. I don't have the compressor with me, so we'll have to tow it." BJ helped her up the high step of the wrecker. "It's too flat to try driving, you could ruin the rim."

His fingers scorched her already hot flesh, warmth flowing through from the inside out. His touch lingered even after she settled into the seat. He frowned and his forehead creased. The man's concern and kindness touched her heart.

"I'm fine. You don't have to worry about me." Jessie tried to hold her skirt together as she climbed into the driver's seat and slid to the center. She placed one leg on each side of the stick shift—a not very ladylike position to be in—but there was a cooler there. Besides, she was more interested in staying as close to him as possible.

"If you say so." He leaned in and flashed a quick smile. His hand now rested on the seat beside her. Brown eyes bore into hers before slowly lowering to her breasts and thighs. He wiped the back of his forearm across his damp forehead. "Well. I better get your car loaded so we can be on our way."

~ *BJ* ~

Bernard Spencer, Jr.—or BJ as everyone called him—admired the curvy woman straddling his stick shift. The glimpse of long, shapely leg encased in thigh highs raised his body temperature a notch. He shifted in the seat. It wasn't just his temperature rising.

He peeked at her again, noting her skirt was torn at the side. What was this lady doing out in the middle of nowhere, looking hot to trot and wearing lace topped thigh-highs? It was summer for fuck's sake, but you wouldn't hear any complaints from him. He'd always had a thing for women in thigh-highs but they only seemed to exist in movies and old Playboy magazines. He gripped the wheel harder. Oh, what he wouldn't give to trail a finger along that lace.

His gaze drifted to the soft flesh visible where her blouse was missing the top button, and a glimpse of a black, lacy bra made his fists clench around the wheel. The woman had obviously been having an interesting day. His balls tightened just thinking about the first time he saw those long legs standing by the car. Fantasizing about her standing there wearing nothing but thigh-highs made him break into a sweat. He turned the air conditioner up a notch.

She looked even better close up. A smile crossed his lips. Her eyes were green with the longest lashes he'd ever seen. Those lips begged to be kissed. His gaze dropped to those gorgeous breasts and there was no way in hell he could look away when she took a deep breath. Those magnificent tits swelled, threatening to pop right out of that little lace bra. He swallowed. The creamy expanse of skin between those hotter-than-fuck stockings and her skirt begged for his touch. BJ had to get a grip. He straightened and squared his shoulders.

Their shoulders touched. He fumbled with the ignition and the truck keys fell on the floor. "Sorry, it's been a long day," he apologized and grabbed for the fallen keys.

"No worries." His passenger exhaled. "Mine's been a trying one as well."

BJ glanced her way and froze. She had the cutest freckles on her nose. Since when did he like freckles? And that hair! Long, thick, and bright red. He'd never slept with a redhead. What color would her nipples be? What was that joke he'd always heard?

Oh, yeah, would the carpet match the drapes? Damn, his jeans were getting tight. BJ shifted in the seat.

He cleared his throat, started the engine, and then reached between her legs to shift the stick into gear. His fingers gripped the gear knob in a death grip. It was just too tempting to not rest his hand on that shapely knee. Or better yet, pull over to the side of the road and have her straddle him. He groaned and switched that hand from the shift to the steering wheel. Better to concentrate on the road than his attractive companion.

BJ had closed his auto repair shop early. There were no more appointments and the one salesman who was coming had called to say he wouldn't make it after all. It'd been a slow afternoon so no sense waiting around for nothing. He had cold beer and bait in the cooler and his fishing pole in the back.

Coming up over the hill and seeing a woman stranded by the side of the road just wasn't in the plans for the evening. He risked a peek at those tantalizing legs of hers of again. Damn, but she was a looker. He'd spied those smoking hot curves a quarter mile away, and her legs grew better looking the closer he drove.

His dick jerked, jumping to life like a divining rod nearing water. If she wasn't married or had some other attachments, he might just get lucky. He'd love to have those gorgeous long stems wrapped around his waist and see her wild hair spread on his pillow as he buried himself deep inside. Taking a deep breath, he tried to calm his beating heart. He'd been avoiding the fairer sex lately and for good reason. They were trouble and couldn't be trusted. He'd learned that lesson the hard way.

Not to mention, he'd just finished closing the deal on a new business. The bank had approved the loan and he'd just signed the lease on a new building. It was not a good idea to have any distractions to get him off track. BJ exhaled as he gave the car's owner another look. Yes, she was hot, but he needed to concentrate on her car and that was all. If he got any more excited, he'd be making an exit from the wrecker with an embarrassing bulge.

The woman had to be a few years older than him. At least it appeared so, since she carried herself with the class and maturity that only years and experience could give. And that voice. Deep and raspy, she'd make a fortune working as one of those phone sex girls he saw advertised on late night television. He couldn't see her doing that, though. This woman practically oozed style, confidence, and sophistication. So different from the women he picked up at the bar when he needed a companion for the evening.

In recent years, BJ had always been honest about not wanting a relationship but, unfortunately, it wasn't what most women wanted to hear. It was getting easier to just jerk off in the shower and spend his evenings alone. He had too much money riding on his future business plans to make stupid mistakes with a young lady looking to hook a husband or make a quick buck.

There was no way, he'd head down that road again. No, he needed to find someone older, established, accepting of him just the way he was but they were few and far between. Could he possibly hope the fiery redhead sitting next to him might be interested in some wild, no holds barred sex and nothing more? Only one way to find out.

CHAPTER TWO

~ *JESSIE* ~

"I'M SO GLAD YOU CAME along. I'm Jessie, by the way." She tried to sound relaxed as BJ reached between her legs, shifting the wrecker into gear. She crossed her arms in front of her, not quite sure what to do with her hands. Every time he moved his foot between the pedals, his leg muscles brushed hers. The small quarters left little room and her left thigh burned from the warmth searing through his dark blue jeans.

Her stomach fluttered with butterflies and a heat settled in her core every time his wrist grazed her knee. She was pressed against him all the way from the toe of her high heeled shoe to her shoulder. The left side of her sizzled at least ten degrees warmer than her right.

"No problem, ma'am. Everyone calls me BJ." He grinned and winked. BJ checked the blind spot and rear-view mirror before hitting the gas.

"Ah. That's an interesting name." And one of her favorite things to give.

"Just a nickname I've had since I was a kid. I was a junior so it was just easier than calling my dad and me by the same name." His hand brushed her knee again, scorching her with his touch. "Unfortunately, the name has stuck to this day." Despite the heat, she swore he had goose bumps rise on his skin before he quickly brushed them away.

Jessie flinched, a spark igniting inside her. Nipples puckered, tight and tender against her lace bra. Her eyes were transfixed by the slender, tan fingers moving between the stick shift and the steering wheel. She ached to have those fingers slide up her thigh and settle between her legs. Jessie swallowed and breathed deeply. The rhythm of her heart beat so fast it would surely leap from her chest any minute.

"I see you have a cooler. I hope I won't be keeping you from a date or anything?" Jessie couldn't believe that just came out of her mouth. She cringed at having sounded like a teenager searching for answers.

"Yep, I got a date, all right."

Jealously spiked at the thought of him making love to another woman. It was silly to say the least. She'd just met this guy, why should she care if he had a girlfriend or not? Still, those eyes had bewitched her faster than anything or anyone ever had.

"I'm sorry for the inconvenience. Hopefully it will only take a few minutes to change the tire and I can be out of your hair in no time." She clasped her hands together and looked straight ahead. Her dreams of any kind of future with the man left back on the road where she'd had a flat.

BJ laughed. "I've got a date with a beer and a fishing pole. How about you? Do you need to call anyone, tell them you'll be late? You should have reception by now." He shifted the stick again, sending another electrical jolt through her system.

"No, I had an appointment but I missed it. I just need to get home and grab some wine, maybe a good book." Damn, Jessie cringed. Had she really sounded that pathetic? So much for being the big seducer. Her lack of social life sounded embarrassing, even to her. Jessie crossed her arms and bit her lip.

She'd been told she looked good for her age. She worked out, did yoga, ate right. Her size six jeans were proof of that. Unfortunately, the few guys she'd come across in the last few years were stuffy, boring, and only looking for a hot piece of ass. Jessie rested her jaw on a fist and stole a quick look at the guy to her left.

Did she dare try to seduce some man she'd just met, let alone someone younger than her? It was a little dangerous to think so, and yet hugely exciting. She'd only ever dated older guys and look how that had turned out. She was still living alone and lonely for love and adventure in her life.

Yes, she deserved to have wild, gratuitous sex with this hot, handsome man. Consequences be damned.

"Well, I'll try to get that tire fixed and have you on your way as soon as possible."

Her heart took a nosedive with his promise for a speedy fix to her car. "Thanks, you've been so kind.

I really appreciate it."

Before she knew it, the vehicle came to a halt. BJ smiled and turned, their faces mere inches apart. His eyes seemed to linger on her lips, and he breathed a deep sigh. Taking a quick glance into his eyes, her senses kicked into overdrive. He smelled so good, so male; an erotic combination of the outdoors, mixed with a hint of musky sweat from the humid day. She could already feel those sensual lips on her mouth, her neck, her breasts, yearning and warmth spread through her body.

Setting the air-brake he put the vehicle in neutral the back of his hand slid across her left thigh. Her muscles quivered at his touch and she craved his fingers to explore more. A shiver ran down her spine.

"Sorry. Not much room in the cab."

"That's alright." Like a footprint in the sand, the impression of his hand on her leg lingered and she tingled all the way to her toes. Hooded eyes rose to meet hers and Jessie couldn't turn away from his stare. Those eyes that appeared dark as coal from a distance now flashed an enticing warm brown. Was that longing? He leaned in. Would he kiss her?

His gaze dropped to her mouth again before he cleared his throat. "Well, ma'am, we're here," BJ announced and exited the truck.

Again the gentleman, he waited to assist her with the long step down. Jessie melted. This man could do anything to her and she wouldn't protest. She wanted him to do anything and everything to her. It didn't matter if it was in the wrecker, on top of the wrecker, on the road. Well, maybe not the road, but a grassy path perhaps. Where had this come from? She never thought this way about strangers.

"Ma'am, are you coming, or do you want to stay out here?" BJ stumbled with the word "coming" and a flush crossed his cheeks.

Jessie looked to where he stood, hand outstretched to help her out of the door. If he only knew how close she was to coming. She smiled and slid across the seat, purposely letting her skirt slide up a little farther. She took the hand he offered. Her eyes were transfixed by her small, fair hand engulfed by his large, tanned one. His fingers warm and smooth, yet rough from hard work. She almost whimpered when he released her hand.

She followed him to the service garage, admiring his firm ass in the tight blue jeans. The overhead sign announced they were at Spencer's, the place she'd been going to pay a sales call. How had she not noticed the same name had been on the door of the truck? The hotness of the truck's driver had distracted her from that detail. BJ unlocked the door, obviously a valued employee since he had his own key. She entered, relieved that old man Bernard seemed to be nowhere in sight.

Her personal mechanic headed for what looked to be an office and returned carrying a folding chair. Opening it, he indicated that she should take a seat. Jessie sat and crossed her legs. Hitting the garage door opener, the big overhead door opened with a rush of heat. The air hung thick from the impending storm. A flash of lightning crisscrossed the sky. BJ headed to a worktable at the back of the garage where he adjusted the channels and volume on a radio. He moved the radio's antenna back and forth until the static cleared.

"I hope you like the blues, ma'am. We don't get too many channels back here."

Jessie nodded her approval. The sultry vibrations of Southern blues serenaded her. It didn't take long for BJ to unload her car, pump up the jack, and start working on her tire. Watching the hunky mechanic work, listening to calming music, and feeling the wild rush of pre-storm air was exciting and nostalgic at the same time. Having grown up in a garage like this, she instantly felt at home. The place was organized, quaint, and had the distinct smell of rubber and oil. A dark patina of grime coated the walls and worktables. A girly calendar and an old timecard machine graced the wall above the radio. Even the *zip-zip* sound of the impact wrench was music to her ears.

Somewhere along the way—she really didn't care when—BJ had shed his shirt. His arm muscles bulged as he pulled off the tire. His sculpted chest glistened, broad shoulders flexed, muscles tightening. Her breasts ached to be pressed naked up against his chest, her body wanted to be held tight in those strong arms. She loved a man with chest hair. Springy black coils enhanced his pecs before tapering to a neat treasure trail heading south. She clasped her hands together, but they still involuntarily wiggled on their own, itching to run their way through the thick, dark curls.

And don't get her started on the tattoos. His skin was a stunning canvas of black ink. A mystery of different designs and images. What she wouldn't give to know the significance of each and every one. Her flesh was marked also, only with much more feminine motifs. It was one of the main reasons she often wore long sleeve blouses and stockings. To cover the different hearts, roses, and other symbols that graced her body. Management frowned on her representing them looking like some biker's old lady. It was a good bet that BJ wouldn't frown at her tats. What else might they have in common?

Jessie had time to think while watching him work. Her mind reeled with plans to lure him to her bed, but she was starting to think that was what he wanted her to do. Maybe she would wait and enjoy the show a little longer. He didn't seem to be in that big a hurry to get the job done.

He checked the air pressure in the other three tires for possible leaks as well. BJ stretched and flexed his muscles several times—not that she was counting or anything. Her concentration broke only a couple of times to listen to the severe weather warnings beeping on the radio.

BJ strutted by her again and returned from the office carrying a big towel. He headed to an outside water pump. Pulling the pump handle up, he splashed water from the hose over his glistening upper body and head. He shook his head sending a spray of droplets in every direction. Jessie smiled as she enjoyed the show. Boldly he glanced her way every so often and flexed a muscle or two. Yes, he was definitely hoping for some kind of response. Her lips twitched holding back her smile. She'd let him beg a little more. The click of the water handle hitting the pump ended his shower. Drying off with the towel, he headed back toward her chair.

His eyes locked on hers, a suggestive smile on his face. "Anything else I can interest you in today, ma'am, since we're already here in the garage? Need any spark plugs, a battery check..." He grinned and raised an eyebrow. "Lube job?" The Southern drawl rumbled slow and exaggerated.

Jessie almost laughed out loud. If she was anymore *lubed up* she'd slide right off the chair. Enjoying the seduction immensely, Jessie shook her head no. BJ strolled over and leaned against the garage door, his left hand rested on his hip. Taking in a deep breath, his jeans slid down a couple inches, revealing dark curls above the top of his now very low waistband. An obvious erection threatened to reveal itself.

A loud clap of thunder caused her to jump. Her heart racing. The air was electric with the ever-nearing storm both outside and inside the building. Jessie swallowed.

BJ glanced at the ground before turning to face her. Thumbs hooked through his belts loops now accentuated his ample package even more. A sexy smirk crossed his lips.

"Ma'am, I think you should probably wait out the storm here. It looks fucking bad." He gazed at the sky before turning back to Jessie. "Ah, I'm sorry about the language, ma'am."

That was it. Jessie uncrossed her legs and sat up

straight. The game had gone on long enough and life was too short to pass up moments like this. It was time to take home the prize, but could she really do it? Step out of her comfort zone for once and go for something she really wanted and what seemed to be being handed to her on a silver platter? Someone unlike anyone she had ever gone for before and seemed to be wanting it as much as she did?

Standing, she walked across the floor, her high heels echoing on the cement. Pasting a determined look on her face, she stopped close enough to feel the heat radiating off his body. Her right index finger poked his chest. "I'll leave when I'm good and ready, and don't you ever fucking call me ma'am again." She poked her finger again for emphasis. "Understood?"

"Yes, mm…ah, Jessie. Sorry about that," BJ stammered, evidently shocked at being put in his place.

"Apology accepted and I happen to like thunderstorms. They're so stimulating, don't you think?" She flashed him her most devilish grin as her fingers trailed across his chest. "Dangerous, powerful, and captivating all at the same time." Under her fingers, his chest muscles tightened.

"Well, Jessie, since you aren't ready to leave yet, what else can I do for you?" He cradled her hand to his chest and his heart beat vigorously against her palm. His skin smooth and warm.

"I can think of a few things," Jessie teased and licked her lips. His sultry gaze fell from her eyes to her mouth. When had she turned into such a femme fatale? Who cared? She loved every minute of her newfound voice. A sense of giddiness and empowerment filled her from head to toe. She felt vulnerable yet in control at the same time.

"Me, too." BJ framed her face with his hands, his mouth lowering to taste hers.

His lips soft yet firm, his kiss both tender and sweet. Her eyes lowered and her knees felt weak. BJ continued to nip at her lips as his fingers slid along her jaw line. He undid the clip of her hair and tossed it aside. Strong fingers glided through the thick strands, slowly untwining it from its French twist.

As the storm intensified, so did his assault on her mouth. Jessie moaned as his tongue slipped in for the first time. He teased and aroused all her senses. His mouth tasted fresh and sweet. BJ's hands slid lower to her waist and her heart rate edged higher.

Finally coming up for air, he found a ticklish spot on her neck with his lips and Jessie giggled, eyes now wide open. A flash of lightning blinded her while thunder shook the ground. The wind belted sand in a dust devil across the road. The sand pelted them from behind. BJ pulled her tightly to his chest, sheltering her from the dirt as he hit the overhead button. The garage door closed and the large building became a private and intimate haven from the storm.

"Don't take this the wrong way but I've been imagining you naked since I first saw you." BJ brushed a piece of windblown hair from her face. His bright smile sent tingles to her toes.

"Is there a right way to take that comment?" she teased.

"I'm hoping so." He picked her up in his arms and carried her to the back of the garage. The lights flickered twice.

"Where are we going? I'm not an engine, you know." Jessie giggled before landing lightly on the clean worktable. Was he going to give her a tune up after all?

"What are you laughing at? I'll have you know I've done some of my best work on this table." BJ laughed, bracing a hand on the counter. "Seriously," he hesitated, "I've always had this fantasy of fucking a gorgeous, hot woman right here on this table." He slid some tools to the side with the swipe of his hand.

Jessie breathed hard. It wasn't just the storm making her nerves feel electrified. He had fantasies and so did she—a younger man for her, a worktable for him. Two birds with one stone, so to speak.

"That sounds like quite the fantasy." Jessie lowered her chin and peeked up. "Has it ever come true?"

"That depends on you." He leaned up and braced a hand on each side of her legs.

"As long as I don't get any splinters." She crossed her legs, posing seductively.

He straightened, a huge smile on his face. "Wait right here." BJ returned to the office and came back with a blanket. The kind you would sit on in the bleachers at a ball game. The colors red and gold. Jessie shifted so he could place it beneath her.

"That's much better. Now where did we leave off?" She placed a finger on her chin. "Oh, yes, you were telling me how good you were with body work."

"Well, first we have to look under the hood." BJ trailed a finger along the neckline of her shirt.

"Whoa. No more car references." Her hand stopped on his chest.

"I'm only teasing you," BJ whispered in her ear, his lips erasing all thought from her mind as he kissed, nipped and licked a trail to a tender shoulder. He slipped buttons from their holes and eased her silk blouse to the side. His finger slid one bra strap down, followed by the other. The wind howled louder rattling the garage walls. All her thoughts merged into one blocking out the storm to center on this young man. His warm, smooth fingers singed her flesh with every touch.

Jessie woke from a passionate haze when he grazed her nipple, his thumb rubbing it to a hard peak. Her pencil skirt slid higher as she wrapped her legs around his waist. She couldn't get close enough. The feel of his cock pressed against her and the new sensation worked its way to her core. The warmth of his hands worked their magic on her breasts. Falling back on the table, she arched her back, her breasts aching for his mouth. A moan escaped as his lips tasted the first bud.

Her fingers ran through his hair and held him close. Her head rolled from side to side as he darted from one luscious peak to the other. If she never left this table, she would die a happy death and call it good. His lips explored down her stomach, licking, nipping, and kissing. No, she wasn't ready to die yet.

He yanked her black lace panties down. His work- roughened hands explored every curve and silky plane of her skin. He squeezed her calf before sliding his hands over her thigh. Her leg trembled with his touch. BJ's whisker-coarse jaw tickled the soft skin of her stomach as he dropped tender kisses there.

He worked his way down. A cry escaped her as his tongue first touched her clit. His mouth explored. He teased her pearl before delving lower to trace his tongue along the folds, rimming her entrance to taste her sweet honey. Inching her body closer to the edge, she craved more.

Her head fell back, the pleasure building higher and higher. Her motor purred to life like a well-oiled machine. Someone had jumped on the gas pedal, full speed ahead. A whimpering sound escaped her lips when he stopped, rose, and silenced it with a kiss. She licked the musky taste of her juices from his lips. His demanding fingers sent her bundles of nerves climbing again, a powerful rhythm matched only by the oncoming storm.

Her chest flushed; muscles clenched. A gasp flowed from her as his finger entered her core. The thrusting fingers twisted, pushing her over a climactic edge. Jessie's toes tingled as flashes of light exploded behind her eyes. The thunder in the background mirrored her ecstasy as it crashed and rumbled through the valley.

One final roar of thunder echoed before a sense of calm filled the air. A light rain now hit the roof. A contented moan sang from her lips. Jessie couldn't remember the last time she'd felt this good, no, this great. She wanted to memorize every detail, every sound, and every smell.

She arched and stretched, fully content, breathing deeply. Sitting up, Jessie wrapped her legs around him. Smiling like a cat with cream on its whiskers, her inner feline meowed for additional treats. She pressed her soft body against his hard one. Her hands trailed down his back before grabbing his firm ass.

Pulling a condom from his wallet, BJ thanked the nail that flattened Jessie's tire. From any direction, she was a work of beauty, her hair a tousled mess. The taste of her still lingered on his lips. The fluorescent lights cast her skin a golden color. He had to look away, catch his breath. Hell, he could shoot a load just looking at her.

Jessie slid off the table, her hands coming to his chest. Her long fingers glided through his chest hair and stopped at the fly of his jeans. The snap popped, the zipper slowly inching its way down. He grasped her hands, no more or he'd explode. Breathing deeply, he turned her around.

"I have to slow down, you overwhelm me," BJ whispered to her back. He held her tightly, his erection pressing her lower back. Kissing her shoulder, he trailed his fingers up her arm. Eying the goose bumps that trailed behind, his chest puffed a little higher. Jessie wiggled her ass, leaning over the counter. *Okay, time's up.* He reached from behind to stroke her clit; her inner thighs drenched.

Never had he met such a stimulating, self-assured woman. Slipping the condom on, he eased gently into her warm pussy. He had her exactly where he wanted; face down on the work bench in his garage, the reality a hundred times better than any fantasy he could remember. Starting out slow, he enjoyed every inch of her slick canal, ever increasing in intensity, thrusting faster and faster. He fingered her clit again. Jessie was already a step ahead quivering on the verge of another orgasm. Her body pressed flat to the table as BJ grasped a handful of her thick red hair.

She cried out, her core grabbing him in a loving grip. BJ gave one last thrust, his body shuddering once, twice, three times. His balls tightened and tingles ran up his spine. A colorful series of fireworks shot through his head and flowed through his veins. He groaned in triumph and came in hot streams. His hand grasped the counter, sure he would pass out from his orgasm.

His other hand reached out and caressed the curve of her hip. Letting out a deep breath, he knew he was lost. Damn. He hadn't pulled out yet and his cock was already twitching for more. He couldn't wait to make love to her again. The next time it would be nice and slow, in his bed, in his home.

CHAPTER THREE

~ JESSIE ~

JESSIE FASTENED THE LAST BUTTON on her blouse as BJ returned from the bathroom. The storm outside had calmed but not her fever for this man.

"So, are you hungry?" He smiled and leaned on the worktable they'd just had sex on.

"You mean, like food?" Jessie raised an eyebrow, sliding her eyes along his lean frame.

"Of course, I mean food." He grinned. "I was going to go fishing but nothing is going to bite after that storm. I just live down the road. I'll grill us up a couple of steaks." He draped an arm around her shoulder and pulled her near.

Jessie had to step away and regain her composure. "That depends. Do you have any workbenches at home?"

"As a matter of fact, I do." BJ kissed the top of her head, his lips nuzzling her ear. "There is also a kitchen counter and lots and lots of tables." He nibbled a delicate spot on her neck.

A smart woman probably would've said no. He could be a serial killer with a padded room at home.

But in this case, she'd plead dumb. Jessie'd felt more alive in the last hour than she had in years. "Lead the way." She smiled. You only live once.

Jessie's car stayed a steady pace behind the wrecker as they pulled down a long driveway. BJ had mentioned he was on call for the evening, but hopefully no one would need his help. The view along the way was gorgeous, it wasn't too far but they had traveled high up a hill. His beautiful, ranch-style home overlooked a lush, tree-filled valley. She parked in front of the garage, got out of the car, and stretched. A shiny black lab came out to greet her, tongue hanging, butt wiggling. She petted his thick, coarse fur and he followed along up the steps to the house.

"His name is Buddy." BJ held the door open for her.

"He's beautiful. I always wanted a dog." Jessie scratched his head, getting licks and a wagging tail in return. "Does he live in the house?"

"At night, during the day he likes to walk around the yard and sleep on the deck. Don't you, boy?" He gave his best friend a pat on the head.

"What a lucky dog." Jessie entered his one-story home. The furniture was masculine yet comfortable. Warm earth tones graced the walls. A beautiful rock fireplace accented one wall along with a couple of deer head trophies. It was cozy and inviting.

She wandered over to the deck he'd just mentioned and slid open the patio door to step outside.

What a sight. The storm had left a double rainbow in its wake. When the sun set in another hour, the view would be amazing. An eagle screeched and soared overhead. She leaned further over the railing, glimpsing the blue outline of the familiar river as it snaked through the trees. Buddy stood beside her his head nudging her leg. Her heart tugged in her chest.

BJ followed her out and brought a lounge chair closer to the railing. "Have a seat and I'll go get the steaks." BJ started the grill before heading inside.

Jessie wanted to help but she couldn't move. The river valley below held all her attention. She had fished that stretch of water many times with her brothers. It was like coming home to loved ones after being gone a long, long time. If the heartwarming feeling only lasted a few hours, it would have to do. She wanted to absorb the moment and every sound, every smell that came with the place.

The patio door slid open and BJ came out toting two beers in one hand, a plate of steaks in another. "All I have is beer. I hope that's okay." Handing her a bottle from a local brewery, he set the plate on a table by the grill.

"Oh, I love this stuff. I worked in their gift shop one summer." Jessie smiled and took a drink.

"Really? I drove a distributor truck of theirs for a while."

"Did you know Rusty?" they both asked at the same time before bursting out in laughter.

"He was quite the character." Jessie frowned and looked in the distance. "I was so sad when I heard he passed away."

"Me, too. My heart broke every time I saw his wife shed a tear at the funeral." BJ turned his attention back to the steaks and added some seasonings.

"You were there?"

"Yeah, and I had visited him a few times in the hospital after his heart attack."

Jessie hung her head. "I was on the road and didn't hear about it until after he had died."

"Theirs was a great love story. We should all be so lucky." He clicked their bottles together in a toast to their lost friend. "To Rusty." He looked to the heavens and returned to the grill.

She felt a lump in her throat and her gaze returned to the valley below. Would anyone be shedding a tear at her funeral? Her brothers probably, but that's about it. She shook her head and stopped feeling sorry for herself. If things were going to change, she couldn't just sit by and wait for love to find her. Jessie eyed BJ before gazing back at the lovely scenery again. Well, he did find her waiting by the side of the road. Was that a sign of good things to come?

A metal tong clanked on the deck floor and jarred her from her thoughts. "Sorry, I should be helping, but it's so lovely out here I couldn't move."

"I'll get it, don't worry." A sizzle sang out as the steaks hit the grill.

Jessie drank her beer, enjoying both the view of the valley and the backside of the chef. BJ retrieved some sweet corn from the house and added that to the grill as well.

A little time later, Jessie set the deck table while BJ finished the steaks. In addition to the steaks and corn, they feasted on microwaved baked potatoes. A generous portion of melted butter and fresh cut chives topped everything on their plates. Spicy ground pepper tickled her nose. A simple meal but one of the best she'd had in a long time. The steak was so tender it melted in her mouth.

Jessie moaned aloud and closed her eyes. Opening them, she watched a trickle of butter slide down BJ's lips as he bit into the juicy cob. She longed to lick that tasty stream of butter from his face. Through the course of the meal, conversation flowed easy. They'd gone to rival schools, had many common interests, and been to some of the same places. How they had never crossed paths before was a mystery. They'd had to somewhere along the line.

After Jessie took the dishes inside, and BJ put the grill away, the sunset took center stage. Standing on the deck Jessie relaxed into BJ's strong arms, swaying back and forth to a silent song. Different shades of orange, amber, and red changed the sky. A lone hawk screeched and flew to its nest.

"You know, the first girl I ever loved had the same color hair as you?" His deep voice sent heat to her core. The Southern drawl conducted shivers along her spine.

"Really," she chuckled, sinking further in his arms, "now that's a story I'd like to hear."

"Well, I was just a kid actually and about this high." He motioned with his hand. "I didn't even know girls existed yet. I was too busy thinking about baseball, riding bikes, stuff like that. Anyway, we stopped at a place to pick up a part my dad needed for a car, and there she was." He gazed off into the sunset.

"There she was? Who was she?" Jessie twisted to stare at his face.

"I have no idea, but as I was waiting in the truck, I noticed this long-legged, young lady walking across the yard. She had beautiful long red hair, wore a tight T-shirt, those really short shorts, and a pair of cowboy boots. It was love at first sight." He laughed and shook his head.

"What did you say to her?" she whispered.

"Nothing. I was scared shitless. If she would have said anything to me, I'd probably have peed my pants." He broke the embrace, leaned against the railing and gazed off in the distance. "I don't know what it was about her, but she gave me wet dreams for a month. Years later, I was driving by that place and I had to stop in." He turned to face her.

"Was she there?" Jessie asked quietly and reached for his arm.

"No, but I asked if anyone knew who she was or where she had gone. One guy thought she was probably the previous owner's daughter but he had no idea what had happened to her. She was at least five or six years older than me so I'm sure she was married with a couple kids by then. Who knows?" He tossed up his hands and smiled.

"Wow, that's quite a story." Jessie flirted. Her breast pressed against his arm. "So, no one has been able to capture your heart since then?" That girl obviously didn't know what a great guy she had missed out on. Her loss, my gain, she thought.

"Nope, she broke my heart." A pained look crossed his face as he grabbed his chest and winked.

"Well, maybe there is something I can do to help you forget her, at least for a little while." Jessie nibbled his ear, sliding her hand up his thigh. Her hands grabbed his firm ass and held him close.

"I don't know. I've been thinking about her for a long..." He pressed his hard length across her stomach. "Long time."

Her eyelids closed a moan escaping her lips.

"It might take all night." He pulled the comb from her hair. She'd put it up after leaving the garage but he obviously preferred it down. His thumb glided along her jaw and brushed across her lower lip. It traveled smoothly around her chin, floated along her neck, and stopped where her pulse beat the strongest.

"I've got all night." Jessie's mind went blank, not sure if she had voiced her opinion out loud or in her head. Her ears burned, heat running through her veins.

His lips followed the trail left by his thumb, nipping along her jaw, sweeping across her lips, nuzzling in her neck. Jessie slipped her hands beneath his shirt, her fingers warmed by the heat of his body. BJ kissed his way to her cheek. His lips brushed her mouth lightly. They played an intimate dance, first waltzing a slow step of nips and caresses before his tongue moved in for a dip. Cradling her head, he wove his fingers through her hair. She moaned and a spasm of pleasure shook her body.

"Are you cold?" he asked with concern, his voice husky. His eyes reflected the moon and shone a golden brown. He rubbed her forearms to erase the goose bumps.

"No, I'm actually very warm right now." She gave a nervous laugh and lifted her lips back to his.

Jessie's tongue invaded his mouth, sweeping across his teeth and worshiping his tongue with hers. A raspy groan rumbled from his throat, sending tingles to every nerve ending. Her nipples peaked as he slowly ran a hand along her side and inside her shirt. Liquid heat spread across her core, she pressed even closer to his hard, lean body. A sweet cry left her lips when he tweaked her aching nipple with his fingers. A cool evening breeze kissed her flushed cheeks. His hand left her breast and pulled her to an awaiting chair.

"Have a seat, Jessie." He held the glider in place as she took a seat. He grabbed a couple of cushions from a nearby chair and kneeled on the deck before her. Jessie's hands reached for his chest as he assaulted her mouth. Her hands eagerly unbuttoned his shirt.

"Don't tell me you always had a fantasy about making love to a woman in this chair," she managed to ask between breathless kisses. Jessie opened her legs and pulled him closer, the cushions putting him at the perfect height.

"I can't say I have, but you seem to inspire me." BJ pulled her legs closer to his body until she sat on the chair's edge. "These fucking stockings, drive me insane."

"I'm glad you like them. Stupid dress code requires me to wear nylons but they're too damn hot. Also can't show tattoos so long sleeves."

"Lose the shirt, keep the stockings," BJ insisted.

She tossed his shirt aside and her blouse quickly joined it on the floor. He unzipped his pants and slipped a condom onto his stiff penis. He was magnificent. She couldn't wait to feel him inside her again. Her soaked panties shoved aside, he thrust in to the hilt. His heavy cock filled her to stretching. She cried out in pleasure, her head falling back as he kissed below her ear. Thick strands of curls caressed her naked back. Long legs wrapped around his waist and pulled him closer.

BJ grasped the edges to slide her back and forth. The chair squeaked like the springs of a bed. Jessie moaned, the slow movement rubbing her G-spot at the perfect angle, the veins and ridges of his dick rippling along that sensitive place.

BJ increased the speed of the chair and then slowed to a stop. She clenched her core and held him deep within. He kissed her tenderly. Jessie purred. Her thighs trembled and she threaded her fingers through his soft hair. BJ deepened the kiss and moaned. A tranquil breeze cooled her feverish skin while a whippoorwill called to its mate.

Breaking the kiss, BJ captured her half-opened eyes and drew her slender finger to his mouth. He kissed the tips before gently sucking first one and then two. "Are there any parts of you that don't taste delicious?" he baited.

"I don't know, I guess you will just have to keep searching and find out." Jessie's voice was a raspy whisper.

BJ kissed her forehead and the rocking continued again. The motion started out slow and built in intensity, his cock sliding back and forth with renewed vigor. Her toes numbed. Her thighs tensed. She gripped his shoulders in a desperate hold as he pounded. She balanced on the edge of orgasm, ready to take flight. Fireworks exploded behind her eyes and her cries of pleasure shattered through the quiet evening air.

BJ clutched the chair with a heavy grip as he lunged deep inside her. An animalistic groan bellowed forth as he came. They clung to each other to keep from collapsing, her body still vibrating as he held her close.

"Fuck, I don't know what it is about you, but in the last couple hours I've had the two best orgasms of my life." His head rested on her shoulder his words muffled by her neck. He hugged her close. She could feel his rapid heartbeat and labored breathing. "Stay with me."

The Southern drawl sent shivers all the way to her little toe. Her heart beat loudly. For the first time in her life, words failed her. She nodded her head, yes instead.

"Good." Rising, he lifted her with him and set her on her feet. He clasped her hand and led her inside. "Buddy, come."

The toenails and dog pads echoed across the

deck as he hurried in for the evening. The patio door closed, the lock clicked.

Jessie followed him into the living room. The house was quiet with the sounds of nature left outdoors. Her body still hummed from their love-making. "I need to take a shower." It had been a long day. She wanted to smell and feel clean again. They let go of hands and he kissed her forehead.

"Just down the hall, towels are in the closet. Help yourself to anything you need." BJ grabbed food for Buddy and filled his water dish. The lab eagerly enjoyed his meal, his dog tags clanking on the side of the stainless-steel bowl.

Jessie kicked off her shoes. Her toes sank in the plush carpet along the hall. It was a welcome massage to her aching feet. The bathroom was paradise and included a huge tub, big enough for two. The large window would give a great view of the countryside to anyone lucky enough to be soaking there in the daylight. Jessie caught a glance of her reflection in the mirror.

Her face glowed, her lips swollen and red. She looked and smelled like sex. A sense of power overwhelmed her. Even if they never saw each other again, she would always remember this feeling. She'd gone after a man she wanted and he was hers, at least for the night. A man so different than any she'd ever met before and had the most amazing sex of her life with. She could do anything, be anything. If only this feeling could last forever.

She removed what little clothes she still had on and entered the huge walk-in shower. The kind of shower she would have chosen for herself if this were her home. Several large showerheads above and to the side, inundated her with warm pulsating water. The soft water rubbed her muscles and caressed her skin. Jessie chose the least masculine-smelling shampoo on the shelf and lathered her hair.

She jumped when large hands worked the shampoo into her scalp. "What took you so long?" she taunted.

Fingers threaded through her wet locks and worked their way down her neck before grasping her wet breasts. Arms embraced her from behind. The feel of his thick erection pressed up against her lower back shot waves of desire through her core. Her hands rested on his as they rubbed and kneaded every curve and plain of her chest.

Their hands moved as one as he stroked her skin and fondled her breasts. Jessie lit on fire, her body humming. Her eyes closed. His wet body slid back and forth from behind, his penis nestled between her ass cheeks. Crisp chest hair brushed along her smooth back as he held her tight, the water unable to flow between them. He pulled her to the tile bench where the water wasn't as strong and placed her on his lap. He kissed her shoulder and stroked her breasts. He grabbed a condom that was sitting nearby on the bench and slid it on.

"You are one sexy woman." He pulled her tight and she gyrated. "I'm sorry but I can't get enough."

"Never be sorry about that." She wasn't.

Jessie rose up and impaled herself on the stiff

length, a reverse cowgirl riding her powerful steed. The position titillated her G-spot, shooting shock waves to her fingertips. His hands helped her bounce up and down. Their moans entwined in the shower, combining with the trickle of the water echoing like a private waterfall. Her head fell back on his shoulder and her hair fell over his back.

BJ's calloused fingers teased her most sensitive spots. Heat flooded her chest and coursed over her skin, ignited nerve endings she never knew were there. Her legs tensed and her hips bucked as her core contracted in climax. BJ followed along the trail of her orgasm, his groan joining hers in trib-ute. Coming down, she was weak as a wet noodle only held upright by his embrace. She wiggled on his lap as one last spasm shook her body to its soul.

"Damn," he howled and held her snug against his chest.

Jessie turned and their foreheads met. Sweet lips grazed his, rubbing softly. He brushed his hand along her neck, his touch intimate and gentle. He nipped her lips before leaving a trail of little kisses behind. Her eyes half-closed. The tender assault caressed her heart and peacefulness settled over her. Steam floated in the air as water trickled down the walls of the shower. Their own private waterfall sheltered from the world.

"You are so beautiful," BJ whispered in her ear. His hand smoothed her hair.

Jessie opened her eyes and rose from his lap to take in every inch of his lean form. If a man could be called beautiful, he was. Her fingers pushed a stray piece of hair out of his eyes and rounded the curve of his face. They trailed along his whisker-covered jaw and down his neck. She rounded a strong shoulder and paused to feel his huge biceps. He laughed and kissed her cheek.

Her fingers spread out upon his chest, the hair springy and wet. Her hand massaged back and forth before stopping to tweak his nipple. His stomach was rippled and smooth. BJ pulled the condom off his shaft and tossed it aside. Her hand inched lower and trailed the length of his thigh. Jessie moved to kneeling, her hands reached for his penis, limp from their lovemaking but still huge to the touch.

She kissed the tip and smiled. "What do you say? Should we try the bathtub next?"

CHAPTER FOUR

~ *JESSIE* ~

JESSIE AWOKE SLOWLY, WARM AND cozy in the big bed. Visions of what BJ had done to her in the bed, on the deck, the shower and in the bathtub still floated through her mind. Had it been a dream? She didn't want to wake up if it was. Her body throbbed and warmth flowed through her veins. She beamed and stretched, feeling for BJ but her hand met emptiness and still-warm sheets. Sighing, she hugged his pillow and inhaled the masculine scent. It hadn't been a dream. Her body tingled with delicious soreness, additional proof he'd claimed her many times throughout the night.

Something tickled her toes...no...licked her toes. The tongue dipped between as teeth glided over her sensitive flesh. Pots and pans rattled in the kitchen, so it couldn't be BJ. She squealed and jolted upright. The black lab at her feet wiggled his tail and panted.

"Bud, come here," BJ ordered from the other room.

The dog bounced off to heed the call of his master. She eased back into the comfort of the bed and rolled to her stomach, lazy and content. The delicious smell of bacon frying assaulted her nose and made her stomach growl. She loved bacon. Covers tossed to the side, she extended her arms and rolled her naked body to the side of the bed.

"Wow, that's a sight I could get used to seeing in the morning." BJ leaned against the doorway.

Her heart thumped and her cheeks flushed. How could he look this gorgeous first thing in the morning? His hair was uncombed, messy, and begged to be touched. He was naked to the waist and a pair of flannel drawstring pants hung from his lean hips. She could see his cock spring to life under the soft, thin fabric. She licked her lips. He crossed the floor in bare feet and stopped near her side to drop a light kiss on her shoulder. Her pulse quickened. "I'm sorry Buddy woke you up. I wanted to surprise you with breakfast in bed."

He could cook breakfast, too? This guy was too good to be true. Her smile grew even bigger. "He licked my toes."

"Well, obviously he thinks you taste as good as I think you do." His finger traced a line up her arm. "I better leave now or I'll burn the house down." He pressed his lips to hers before heading back to the kitchen.

Jessie tried to regain her composure, willing the rapid beat of her pulse and her tortured breathing back to normal limits. She scanned the room. Her discarded clothes were nowhere to be found, so she surveyed his closet and chose a grey T-shirt to wear.

The savory smell of fresh brewed coffee enticed her to the kitchen. BJ stood at the stove, a dish towel thrown over one shoulder. "How do you like your eggs?"

"I'd love some sunny side up. I'm terrible at making eggs, mine always turn out scrambled." She wrapped her arms around his waist.

"I can do eggs and bacon but that's about it for breakfast food." He cracked a brown egg one-handed and dropped it into a fry pan.

"Is that coffee I smell?" Her eyes scanned the kitchen.

"Sure, right over there." He pointed to the coffee machine and cracked another egg into the pan.

Jessie poured herself a cup as her breakfast companion finished up the meal. BJ placed the eggs and meat on plates before carrying their servings to the patio.

As they exited the house, two cardinals flew from the bird feeder. He set their dishes on the deck table while Jessie followed with their coffee and juice. They settled down to eat and enjoy the morning view. It was all too surreal, like they were some old married couple that had been doing this for years.

"So, do you like baseball?" He pointed his fork at her T-shirt.

"Yes, I guess so. Why do you ask?" She bit into a piece of bacon.

"The shirt you chose. It's the West Virginia Express team. I thought maybe you were a fan or something."

"Oh, I never looked. I just grabbed the first one." Jessie pulled the shirt front out and looked down. "I used to go with my brothers, but I haven't been to a game in years." She waved her fork and stabbed a helping of eggs. "You know how it is. They get married and have their own lives. They're so busy I hardly ever see them. What about you? Are you a baseball enthusiast?"

"Yeah, I go once in a while and I actually have tickets for tomorrow's game. Do you want to go?" He asked a hopeful smile on his face.

Jessie stopped chewing and watched him run a hand through his hair. Was he asking her out on a date? Her inner voice screamed yes, go for it. They would get to spend some more time together and see where things went after that.

"Sure, that would be fun." She crossed her legs and swung her foot, unable to stop the happiness from bubbling up to her wide smile. He wanted to spend another day with her. And she wanted to spend every minute of the weekend with him. Could the day get any better? "But I better get going. I'm sure you have a lot of things to do today."

Jessie twiddled her fingers under the table. The thought of returning to her empty apartment held no appeal. She should go see her dad but last time they'd talked he said Travis was keeping him busy and insisted she take some time to relax.

"You said you used to fish." BJ tapped his index finger on the side of his coffee mug.

"Yes. I loved it. Used to go catfishing all the time. My mom hated us kids coming home smelling like stink bait though." Those were good memories and times she'd never forget.

"Well, I . . ." BJ shrugged his shoulders and glanced off in the distance, "I was going fishing last night but with the storm and all…" His faced blushed when he said 'and all'. "Thought maybe I'd try my hand at it today." His gaze returned to hers. "Care to come along?"

"Ah, sure. I'd love that. I just need to get my bag out of the car so I can change."

"Do you want me to get it for you?" BJ started to rise. He really was a southern gentleman.

"No, no. Please sit and enjoy your meal. I just need to grab a few things, so no big deal."

The man across from her settled back in his chair. After she said yes, he seemed to relax. Buddy wandered over and his owner scratched his head. "What do you say, Bud? You want to go for a boat ride?" The dog pranced. His big tail hit the metal table with a big thump, thump. "It's a deal then. We'll go as soon as you're done eating and I'll get the boat packed while you get ready."

"Looking forward to it." Jessie took a sip of her coffee. She could get used to spending time here. Very used to it. Right now, she never wanted to leave.

~ BJ ~

He'd be lying if he said he didn't enjoy having

Jessie around and it scared the hell out of him. Not that he was scared of her, no she was soft, warm, and made him feel fuzzy all over. It was the emptiness that would follow once she left that had him uneasy.

His experience with women, well particularly one woman, had him gun-shy of everything in high heels and a skirt. There was a knot in his stomach just thinking that Jessie might be the same way but it would be too much to hope for that she wasn't. But still…

BJ didn't like stereotyping everyone into one category but he'd been hurt one too many times. Well, not that many but once was enough. That experience kicked him in the heart and kneed him in the balls.

He relived the experience while gathering poles, bait, and a cooler for the boat. Ashton was his college sweetheart. Blond, beautiful, and they had everything in common, or so it seemed. Moving in together their senior year was an exciting time.

One day he left their place to go to class but had forgotten his laptop. BJ tried to be quiet as he walked back in not wanting to wake her but Ash was up and talking on the phone.

Hearing his name, made him stop short. Ashton was talking to a friend about them. Expecting to hear good things, her comments cut to the core. It was his home they were staying at and she expressed in no uncertain terms that that was the only reason she was there. BJ had to admit that he was paying most of her way but he never thought of it like that.

If you cared about someone, you did everything you could to help them. She then went on to say, that once they were married, she'd never have to work. Ashton was almost ready to graduate with a nursing degree, why wouldn't she want to use it? They hadn't even talked about marriage and she was already planning her life as a trophy wife! What the fuck? How could he have been so blind? He fell against the wall as he continued to listen as she stated his many faults.

Ashton had used him and he'd let her. The more he thought of it the more BJ realized things he didn't want to admit. Money that had gone missing from his wallet. Things that seemed to disappear from his truck or apartment. She was a thief and the worst kind. The bitch had stolen from his heart and his home.

After that, he closed down, work was his constant companion. His bank account had soared and so had business. Women were off his radar and he never got involved with them for more than one night. Never letting his guard down for a pretty face, until yesterday.

Maybe it was the storm, maybe he'd just had a weak moment but here he was and here she was. Jessie whistled a tune as she walked his way. Her hair tucked up in a trucker's hat and wearing shorts, a t-shirt, and cowboy boots. Something about the look calmed his nerves and seemed familiar but those thoughts quickly diminished.

Her bright smile lit up her face and he locked it

down to memory for a cloudy day. It was a given she was a career woman. Someone that didn't need a country boy holding her back, but he would take every minute he could get before they went their separate ways.

CHAPTER FIVE

~ BJ ~

DESPITE STOPPING AT THE LOCAL bait shop, it didn't take long to get all their gear in the back of the truck and drive to the boat landing. Jessie knew what to do without being told and they easily had the boat in the water in no time at all.

He waited for Jessie to take a seat before pushing off from the dock. A quick turn of the key on the surface drive and they were on their way. Finally finding the deep bend that he wanted to fish, he killed the engine and dropped anchor.

While he did that, Jessie already had the stink bait she'd bought open and was dipping her sponged hook inside. BJ could smell the stench that catfish loved from where he sat but she didn't bat an eye. It was nasty and smelled like a combination of raw chicken, blood, and old cheese that had been left out in a bucket to simmer on a hot summer day.

"Smells bad but the kitties love it." She glanced up at him and winked.

"I'll take your word for it."

"You don't believe me, do you?" Jessie smirked.

"No, it has to work or they wouldn't sell it but nothing beats fresh meat." He opened a blue plastic container and dug around for a fat worm.

"Yuck. I hate those things. I know they will like my bait better." Jessie released the catch on the fishing reel, drew the pole back, and cast. The heavy lure made a plunk noise as it hit the water and sank to the bottom.

"I'm thinking you just threw out a challenge."

"By the look of those skinny night crawlers you're using, it won't be much of a battle," she teased.

"I'll have you know it doesn't matter how skinny the worm is, it's how you use your pole," BJ countered.

"Ha, are we still talking about fishing?"

"Just putting a spin on that old saying about the boat and the motion of the ocean." He winked her way.

"All I know is that you're not going to catch anything with your line still in the boat."

"Very true." He cast his line in a different direction.

"So what are the rules and prizes of this fierce fishing tournament I just got myself into?" He knew the river like the back of his hand so wining would be easy.

"Biggest fish out of five wins," Jessie answered.

"And the loser has to do what?" BJ hoped it involved anything that would cause Jessie to be naked. That made him feel like a horny teenage but so be it. Around her, he was.

She chewed her lips for a moment before answering. "Loser cooks supper."

"Sounds like a plan. I know I can cook but what about you?"

"Too bad you won't be finding out anytime soon." The tip of Jessie's fishing pole started to jerk up and down. It was a catfish. "I got my first one." She yanked the pole up and hooked the fish. For the next minute, Jessie expertly reeled the fish in. Not pulling too hard but keeping enough tension on the line to not lose him.

"I'll get the net." BJ held it out and easily scooped up her fish as it popped about the surface. "Nice one." It was a perfect eater but wouldn't be taking first prize if he had anything to do with it. "He's a keeper." BJ carefully removed the hook from the fish and placed him on ice in the cooler.

"The next one will be bigger." Jessie pouted but there was determination in her posture as she put more bait on the hook and cast it out again.

"Hey!" His pole started to thump up and down. It was a cat for sure and a big one. "Now it's my turn." This fish was huge. As soon as he reeled, the fish would go back down and pull out line. It took several minutes for him to tire the fish out. When it finally came up to the boat's edge, they both gasped. It was a monster cat. The thing was the size of a log.

"Damn, there's no way I will be able to get him in the boat." Jessie had set her pole down to hold the net but that fish wouldn't begin to fit in that.

BJ knelt by the side of the boat and grabbed the

giant fish by the gill. "This old girl's not going any-where." He eased the hook out and gently moved the tired fish in the water to get more oxygen in its gills. This fish had too many years on it to be worth eating and deserved to finish out its life in the mucky depths. When she regained her strength, BJ let her go. The big blue cat finally swam away and dipped back to the murky depth. "I caught one a few years ago, a buddy of mine had a scale and we weighed it at forty-eight pounds."

"That's crazy. I've never seen anything that big. Too bad you didn't keep it, you'd have won." Jessie sat back down and began to reel another one in. They had definitely found the honey hole.

"There's more to life than winning. That fish was old, not worth eating, and probably still had a few good years left in her."

Her deep green eyes met his. "I like the way you think. Even if I do win, I might decide to cook for you anyway." Her pause caused the fish she was reeling to get loose. "Damn. Lost it."

"Either way, I'm a winner for getting to spend more time with you." Whoa, where did that come from? BJ reached for a bottle of water from the cooler. He must be getting lightheaded to say something as lovesick as that.

Jessie's mouth opened but no words came out. She just looked at him, her expression unread-able. Great, he'd put his big fat foot in his mouth and now things were awkward. As soon as they returned to the dock, Jessie would probably hit the road. *Way to go, dumbass.*

"You got a bite." She pointed to the pole dancing in his hands.

"I do." BJ reeled another catfish in. This one about the same size as Jessie's if not a hair bigger. "So how many do you want to keep?"

"Well, the contest was for the best out of five. We each have one so we need four more." As she spoke, another one tugged at her line.

At least she didn't ask to go in after his lovesick confession. He needed to be more laid back for the rest of the time or he'd scare her off. Heck he was scaring himself. She was just passing through. Jessie had briefly mentioned she traveled for work. There was no future for them and what about what happened with Ashton? Was it time to let that go and give a relationship a chance?

"Can you get the net?" He'd just caught another.

"I got it. Just reel him in and I'll grab him." She did as told.

They seemed to have found a hole of fish that were of similar size. He reached for the cat, watchful of the sharp spines on the fish's fins. Catfish had three and he'd learned the hard way to be cautious of those things. It made the funny noise that catfish do. A kind of a cross between a pig grunt and a bark.

Her laugh did strange things to his heart. It fluttered and he almost dropped the fish.

"I'd forgotten about the goofy noise they make. Boy does this bring back good memories of fishing with my dad and brothers." Jessie clasped her hands together in front of her.

For a brief moment he pictured a couple kids in the boat with them, a girl with red pigtails and a dark-haired boy pulling worms out of a bucket to scare his sister. Dammit, he needed to get a grip. If he didn't control his emotions soon, he'd be down on his knee promising marriage. "Yeah, it's a nice day. We only have a few hours so you better keep fishing."

"Yes, and someone will have a lot of fish to clean and cook tonight and it won't be me," Jessie challenged again.

"We'll see about that," BJ rallied back. He liked this girl. He liked her a lot. When he'd spied her tattoos last night he was in heaven, if she was into motorcycles he might just be in love.

Hours later, they'd compromised. BJ cleaned their catch while Jessie worked in the kitchen. As soon as he finished, he cleaned up by the water pump before bringing them inside to see what she'd come up with.

"Well what did you find?" He almost stopped in his tracks. Jessie had taken a quick shower and washed her hair. It may be his shampoo but it never smelled this good on him. Her long legs were even tanner after the afternoon in the sun. She wore a simple sundress, yellow with white flowers here and there. Buddy was laying at her feet. Usually he liked to lick the fish before BJ cleaned them but not today. The canine couldn't leave her side.

"What's wrong?" Jessie tilted her head and poked out her lower lip.

"Nothing. I'm just not used to having such a

pretty guest in my kitchen. You clean up pretty good for a fisherman."

"Ha. You're not so bad yourself when you're not smelling like stink bait." She walked over to give him a kiss but he stepped to the side.

"I do smell like fish guts and I don't want to get your pretty dress dirty." She wasn't taking no for an answer and pulled him in a for a kiss anyway. This woman was proving to be a no holds barred girl and he liked it.

After they came up for air, she took the bowl from his hands. "I got things handled if you want to get cleaned up."

"Are you sure?" He wasn't used to having someone offer to help with things.

"Yes, now go." Jessie put the bowl down and started dipping the filets first in a bowl of milk and then the breading. He started to leave but stopped when he heard the fish sizzle when she laid them in the pan.

"Hey, Jessie?"

"Hmm?" She pushed a strand of hair out of her face with the back of her hand.

"I'm glad you're here." His voice came out lower than he planned. With more feeling than he planned.

"Oh, yeah." Her hands stilled. "I'm glad I'm here also but I should probably get going before it gets too late."

Not if he had anything to do with it. BJ stepped closer. His front pressed to her back. "I want you to stay."

"Oh, yeah?" Jessie said again before twisting to face him. "I should really get home but I could be persuaded to stay a bit longer."

He pulled her tight and her eyes widened. There was no question that he desired her with his hard as a rock length pressed against her stomach. "Is this long enough for you?"

Her laugh lightened the moment. "Yes, very but that doesn't mean that I still can't use some per-suading."

"I plan on making it worth your while. All. Night. Long." BJ bent his head to drop kisses along her neck. Her scent a combination of sunshine, fresh air, and cooking spices.

"I like the sound of that."

CHAPTER SIX

~ BJ ~

BJ CROSSED HIS ANKLE OVER his knee and slid down in the stadium chair. He liked living alone, always had. So why had sharing breakfast with Jessie this morning felt so right? He inhaled a deep breath as warmth spread down his back. The fact was he wanted to wake up next to her hot body again tomorrow, and the next day, and the day after that. Hell, they'd used up every condom in the house, and his balls still hurt. The sight of her in one of his shirts again this morning gripped his heart like a vise.

Jessie was gorgeous, smart, fun, and yet independent. Call him lovesick and stupid but for the first time in a long time, he had a good feeling about a woman. That there was a possible future and that he'd be batshit crazy to let her just walk out of his life.

BJ took a deep breath. He had to slow down and think things out. He knew every inch of her stunning body like the back of his hand but he really knew nothing about this woman. The thought hit him like a sucker punch to the stomach. BJ watched her take a bite of her hotdog, lingering as her tongue licked a smudge of ketchup from her lip. His cock stiffened and he fanned himself with the game program.

"How's your hotdog?" He smirked, asking the question when she had her mouth full.

"It's delicious." Jessie swallowed her food and laughed. "I haven't had this much fun in years. Thanks for bringing me here today." She dabbed her mouth with a napkin before kissing him on the cheek.

"Jessie, how's a great person like you not married? Or is there a big boyfriend around here that I have to worry about?" He motioned to the crowd before placing his hand on her thigh.

"No boyfriend, no husband. I work a lot. I'm on the road all the time so it's hard to keep a relationship going when you're never in town. What about you?" Her green eyes locked onto his.

"Same here, I'm a workaholic—at least I have been in the past. I saved a long time to get enough money to buy my house Now I'm finishing a project that I've been working toward for a long time. Once I get that up and running, who knows?" He did know. He wanted a partner in life, maybe even someone that would help run the business. A company they could build up and pass down to their children. And at this moment, she seemed like a pretty good part of that plan… but would Jessie want the same things?

"That's very impressive? How old are you again?"

"I never said but I'm twenty-nine. I won't ask

you because a gentleman never asks a woman her age." He winked.

She smiled at the answer but the shocked expression on her face when he said his age couldn't have been missed. He didn't care about age differences and Jessie shouldn't either. "Do you think you will be on the road forever?" There had to be a way for them to be together.

"Well, that all depends on Bernard." Jessie bit into her meal again.

Huh? "What did you say?" Did she want him to ask her to stay? He ran a hand through his hair and sat a little straighter.

"Your boss, Bernard Spencer. That's who I was going to see when my car got a flat."

Did he hear her right? His palms started to sweat. Come to think of it, he never told her that was his full name. What business did she have with his father?

"You think my boss is Bernard?" He regarded her out of the corner of his eye.

"He owns the garage, doesn't he?' She took the last bite of her dog.

"Well, yes, but why were you on your way to see the owner of a garage?" Warning bells rang in his ears, why would she be coming to see him?

"I'm a salesperson for Bauer's Auto Parts. I was just making a routine sales stop, but when I heard that he was going to be starting a business in Charleston, heck, I thought I'd go for broke and ask him for a job." She dabbed her mouth with a napkin. "I heard through the grapevine he was looking for a manager. I've saved up money, maybe he would even let me invest." She shrugged her shoulder. "Who knows I might like staying around. I know my family would like me to stay. I certainly have missed a lot by being gone."

Jessie watched the game beside him but she spoke as if she was miles away. "I can't even have plants as they die on me. It's a long shot, but I thought I would give it a try."

BJ remembered a voicemail left on the machine from someone named Jessie. Hell, with that sultry low voice of hers, she sounded like a man on the phone. If she was who she said she was, it would be a miracle. He did need a manager. Hell, he hadn't gotten around to hiring any employees for the store yet. Then again, things just didn't fall into his lap like this. Was this just the luck of the draw that she ended up with a flat tire or had he been set up?

People would do anything to get ahead these days but the last thing he wanted to do was get involved with someone and lose his heart or more. Been there, done that. His heart and bank account took a hit that left both empty for a long, long time. It would be a cold day in hell before he'd make that mistake again. If only there was a way to find out if Jessie was here for the right reasons and not just getting closer to him to gain a position at his business. A test of some sorts but that seemed cold and heartless.

Hopefully it would come to him in the next few days. Something that would benefit both of them whether it would push them together or pull them apart was yet to be seen. He frowned on romances in the workplace. That often led to more trouble than it was worth and there a clause in place just for that very reason.

He hated to mistrust people, but scam artists were everywhere. He had too much money set aside to gamble it away on someone just because they set his dick on fire. Not that it had ever happened to him, but you never know. Wait, didn't he know someone at Bauer's? Yes, Brad Johnson, they'd gone to high school together. First thing tomorrow morning he would make some calls, check her out. He curled his left hand around the armrest and crossed his fingers.

If worst came to worst, he might hire her but it may also end whatever future they could've had. It may come down to him or the job, whatever she chose to do. His head hurt just thinking about it. If that was the case, he'd enjoy every moment they had left together. Jessie was used to being on the road, maybe she never meant to stay away but a long-distance relationship held no appeal for him.

"I thought you liked traveling. Being on the road and such?" BJ gripped the arms of his chair. A chill going down his back on this warm day.

"I do and I can't wait to leave again but my dad's in poor health right now. I need to be close to home until he can get back on his feet again. I love my job but I love my father more. Who knows maybe I will want to stay permanently."

He respected that but it didn't dull that ache that she was still thinking about passing through even if she did get a job nearby. How long would she stay?

"What do you think? I hate to ask but do you know if he has hired anyone yet?" Her face looked sad and vulnerable. "I hope we aren't up for the same job."

"No, we aren't up for the same job, but I have to ask. What kind of experience do you have for running an auto supply business?" BJ looked her straight in the eye and searched for answers.

"I grew up in the business. My dad owned Sparky's Repair Shop. I knew how to change the oil in a car before I was ten."

"Wait a second." His heart skipped a beat and he couldn't catch his breath. "You're Sparky Knutson's daughter?" Was she the one he remembered seeing from his dad's pickup truck so many years ago? Could she be the one? They did have the same color hair and she hadn't mentioned having any sisters.

"Yes, my brothers did most of the work, while I got stuck doing the paperwork and accounting. I ordered supplies, did payroll, advertising, cleaning. You name it, I did it." She smiled before frowning. "Unfortunately, my dad's heart wasn't in it anymore with all of us gone so he retired early. Neither of my brothers wanted to take over so he sold the business and bought a little place out in the country." Jessie took a sip of her soda and placed it in the cup holder.

"I got hired at Bauer's and I've been working there ever since, but this would be a great opportunity for me to use the experience I have and also get more women involved in the business. I would like to offer some night classes for women on general automotive maintenance and what to do in an emergency." Jessie snuggled closer and clasped his hand in hers. "You know, in case a handsome mechanic with a wrecker doesn't come by when you need him."

BJ had to admit, she did have good ideas. He never would have thought to do classes. "Well, that all sounds good. I know I'd hire you on the spot." He did want to hire her, but he had to be sure. That meant checking out a few things first. There were several things at play and it wasn't just her ability to do the job.

What happened when her father regained his health? Would she be on the road again and take his heart with her? "Why don't we just enjoy the day and see what happens tomorrow?" A loud crack of the bat sent their gazes back to the field. The players raced around the bases and the crowd rose to their feet.

"Woohoo. A triple play, we won, BJ. We won!" Jessie stood and threw her arms around him. "Thank you for bringing me here today. I had a great time."

Her soft breasts pressing against his chest was the equivalent of hitting a home run. He crushed his lips on hers and his tongue weaved an erotic dance around hers. BJ pulled her closer to the erection growing in his jeans.

"Hey, BJ, get a room." His passion was interrupted when a piece of popcorn hit his cheek.

"What the fuck?" He searched the crowd behind them. His gaze landed on two laughing guys in the back row he knew from the local gas station.

"Let's finish this at home." He whispered in her ear while giving the hecklers a one-finger salute behind her back. Oh, the harassment he'd be receiving from those two the next time he needed fuel. BJ smiled. It would be worth every second of teasing.

CHAPTER SEVEN

~ *JESSIE* ~

JESSIE EYED THE DASHBOARD CLOCK, the time passing too quickly. She ran her hand along BJ's thigh, feeling the muscles move as he transferred from the gas to the shift pedal.

"Damn, I almost forgot." BJ hit the signal lever and entered the drug store parking lot.

"What's wrong?" Jessie looked around the parking lot.

"I've got a hard-on and we're out of condoms." He put the truck in park and ran a hand through his hair.

"Is that all? I can help you with that." Jessie unbelted her seat belt and reached for his zipper.

"Damn." He drove a little way away from the store and put the truck in park.

Excitement flowed through her veins, eager to put her lips on him. Heat swirled to her center as she freed his swollen cock from his jeans. He was hard as steel, but smooth to the touch. Her fingers glided along the side of his solid shaft, across the velvet head, and down the other side to his balls. She smiled. Grasping his hard length in one hand, she pumped in long sensual strokes. Their gazes held and she lowered to take him in her mouth. He was so big. She took as much as she could in and lightly traced her teeth along his tight skin on the way up.

BJ groaned. His head reclined on the head rest. "That feels so fucking good." BJ entwined his fingers in her hair, his breaths labored.

She couldn't help but look up. He was so handsome. That she was the cause of his pleasure thrilled her to the bone. Her pulse raced as she returned to take him full in her mouth. His cock throbbed. Jessie ran her lips up and down, first slow, then fast. Her hand gripped his balls in a tight hold while she stroked his shaft up and down with the other. She drew him greedily down her throat. Desire filled her core.

"Oh, Jessie, I'm going to come."

He struggled to withdraw, but she wouldn't let him leave her mouth. She wanted all of BJ, heart and soul, even if that meant only for a short time. Satisfied, Jessie let his spent penis fall from her lips with a victorious smile. Leaning in, she grabbed his jaw and crushed his lips with hers. Shivers ran down her spine. She liked him, a lot. The endless travel was looking less and less appealing. There was something about this man that made her feel like she belonged.

"I could use a few things also. I'll get them and be right back." She crawled out of the truck to head to the store. Her legs wobbly and her heart in turmoil. Just being near him, had her whole system out of whack.

What if Bernard didn't hire her? He just had to. She wanted to stay and not just because of her dad. There had to be some way to hopefully make something work with BJ. It had started out as just wild sex in a garage, but that no longer seemed enough. Her lower lip pouted. It would be wonderful to have someone like him to come home to every night, not for just one night. She bit her lip. It was never enough for her mother. Could it be enough for her?

It didn't take her long to find what she needed in the store. The checkout line was thankfully short. She grabbed her purchases and journeyed out in the sunshine. Her spirits lifted as soon as BJ's truck came into view. She climbed in and set the stuffed bag between them.

"It looks like you got more than a box of condoms." BJ shifted the truck into gear and set off for the highway.

"Well, there was a movie that just came out that I wanted to see." Jessie looked through her bag of purchases. "I also couldn't watch a movie without popcorn and I bought some things to make s'mores. Too bad I have to go home and watch it all by myself." She didn't want to assume that he would want her to spend yet another night together.

"You're not going anywhere." He reached for her hand and kissed the back of it. "Well, unless you want to. I'm not ready for our weekend to end."

Jessie's heart soared. Was he for real? God, she

hoped so.

As they pulled in the driveway, Buddy greeted the truck with a bark. He circled once before stopping at Jessie's door. She opened the door before BJ had a chance to. Buddy bounced up and down and licked her hand. A cozy feeling shot through her from head to toe. His dog liked her; that was a good sign wasn't it?

"Obviously you have a way with the males in this household," he teased before reaching to carry her bags from the drug store and the game. He had purchased her an Express T-shirt and some souvenirs from the game. "What do you say we take Buddy for a walk?"

"I'd love to."

"Then let's go. I'll take these in the house and be right back."

BJ caressed her palm as he led Jessie through some of his favorite trails in the woods. They quietly watched a deer and her two fawns. They kissed near a small waterfall and stood in awe of a breathtaking view when they reached the high point on their hike. The walk back was easy and all downhill. Jessie's mind tried to memorize all the bits and pieces of their journey, the songs of the birds, the smell of wildflowers, and the feel of his arm draped around her shoulder.

"You are so lucky to live here, it's like paradise." Jessie squeezed his hand and gestured to their surroundings with the other.

"You really think so? I picture you as more of a city girl."

"My dad was a country boy who fell for a city girl who hated it here. We lived in town because of Mom, but any chance I got I would be out fishing or four wheeling with my brothers. I'm still a girly girl, but I love being out in nature." She wrapped her arms around his waist. "Thanks for sharing your home with me for the weekend. You have no idea how much I have enjoyed our time together."

"Well, it's not over yet, so don't start getting all mushy on me already." He hugged her close and kissed her forehead.

Mushy. Well, so much for being Miss Cool and Collected. She basically advertised clingy and desperate right now, her emotions getting the best of her. She wanted that job with Bernard so bad she could taste it. Right now, the reasons why were blurred but did it really matter?

As they continued their walk. BJ pointed out different landmarks and places that he enjoyed visiting, a pond that was good for fishing, an eagle's nest, and a spot Buddy escaped being sprayed by a skunk. The sun started to dip behind a hill as BJ's home came in sight. Would tonight be just as wonderful as the last?

Later that evening, they snuggled in bed as the movie began to play on the flat screen television. A bowl of popcorn nestled between them. Buddy snored on the floor below the bed. Jessie relaxed in his arms, not watching a single moment of the video but instead just enjoying BJ's embrace. For the first time in her life, the man next to her held more appeal than the superstar action man in the film. Way too soon, the closing music score started playing.

"What did you think?" He leaned over to look into her eyes.

"You're..." Her cheeks reddened and she stopped. "Ah...it was wonderful. A great movie, I really liked it." She stuttered, embarrassed to be caught comparing him to a movie and its leading man.

"You are a mystery to me." He placed a kiss on the tip of her nose.

"Who, me? I'm pretty much an open book. What you see is what you get."

"I'm not too sure about that. I think there are many areas of you I haven't begun to see yet." He set the popcorn bowl aside and hooked a finger on the sheet, sliding it lower.

"Really, like what?" Her heartbeat quickened.

"Well, I haven't seen this particular spot behind your ear before." He swept a piece a hair off her neck and dropped a sweet kiss.

"There's also this little hollow along your collar bone." He slid his tongue along the mentioned line. A moan escaped her lips as he nipped a sensitive area. In such a short time, he knew exactly what to do to set her body on fire.

Her eyes slowly closed. Bliss filled her veins and sparks flowed from head to toe. Her arms wrapped around his waist and clutched him tight. BJ's touch sent her on a trip she never wanted to return from. His lips mapped a journey to her breasts, giving each tight peak his loving attention. The heat from his thick length scorched her thigh. His palms pressed her breasts together as he lavished devotion to both tips.

"I can't wait. I have to be inside you." He growled as he touched her folds. His fingers dipped to test the waters that flowed.

"You have me," she whispered in his ear.

BJ tossed the sheets aside and lifted her legs high. He grabbed a condom from the night table and with one powerful thrust, he was home. A cry of pleasure rang from Jessie's throat. Her head swayed and her gaze landed on the closet mirror reflecting their passionate embrace. His body was an erotic celebration of flexing muscles, surmounting any fantasy man she had ever dreamed of. The driving force of his engorged cock filled her to the hilt. Her brain numbed and her eyes rolled back in ecstasy. Jessie gasped and her hips bucked as the scent of their lovemaking filled the air.

"Look at me, Jessie," he commanded.

Her gaze met his. His intense stare took her breath away and she couldn't look away if she wanted to. BJ seized her soul and body and captured her heart. Jessie felt a tear roll down her cheek as he started to stir inside her, at first so slow it was agony and ecstasy at the same time. He dropped a kiss to her heart as his thrusting increased to a frenzied pace. Jessie clutched his lower back. Manicured nails scratched his warm flesh. Tingles of energy filled her core, sending her up a stairway to the stars. Each stroke edged her higher to the top. Her core contracted as her toes tensed. All-consuming passion streamed through her body as flashes of light burst inside her head. He groaned as she cried out.

Static sounded on the TV as the credits came to an end. Tomorrow meant nothing and they were alone in the world. This was what she wanted in life, but not for a weekend, or a week, not even a month. Jessie wanted this feeling to last forever. She just had to find a way to make herself believe it and make it happen.

CHAPTER EIGHT

~ JESSIE ~

JESSIE WOKE TO A WHIFF of bad breath from a panting dog. She stretched and rolled toward BJ's side of the bed. It was cold to the touch. A glass canning jar filled with wild daisies and a note greeted her on the side table. It simply read, 'Be at the garage at 10 to meet Bernard'.

Her shoulders sank. If this was to be her last morning here, it would have been wonderful if they could've woken up, had breakfast, and gone to see Bernard together. Was he going to miss her if she didn't get hired and went on the road again? What about once her dad was better and she left? Jessie sank back into the bed. She would miss him and that was putting it mildly.

When she heard through the grapevine that Bernard Spencer would soon be opening a large auto supply store in nearby Charleston, she jumped at the chance to try to get in on the ground level. Hopefully, he might even consider taking her on as a partner. Maybe it would be great to stay in one place and she was good at her job. Good— hell no, she was great. No one knew more than she did about the auto parts business. If she could just convince him to give her a chance, she'd finally be able to settle down in one place. And she could see where things might lead with BJ.

There was only one thing to do, dazzle Bernard Spencer and get the job. Decision made, she jumped out of bed and into the shower. After a quick breakfast, she chose an ivory-colored blouse and a tan skirt. Strapping on some brown, high heeled sandals, Jessie gave herself a once over in the closet mirror. Tucking her hair up in a clip, she felt professional. Her coworkers labeled her style "class with sass." Taking one last look, she kissed Buddy on the head and headed out the door. Jessie already missed the place and she hadn't even left it.

In no time at all, she arrived at Spencer's Auto Repair. Her gaze landed on BJ's truck and what she had done to him in the front seat bloomed fresh in her mind. Taking one last look in the visor mirror, she took a deep breath and headed for her meeting with Bernard.

"Hello, ma'am, what can I do you for today?" A burly man with a mustache welcomed her as she approached.

"I'm here to see Bernard Spencer." Her voice cracked and she cleared her throat.

"He's in the office, ma'am, right over there." His greasy, rag-filled hand pointed the direction.

"Thanks." She started toward the door and stopped. "Say, is BJ around?" She didn't want to be sent on her way without saying goodbye first.

Greasy-hand-man pointed again without looking up. "He's in the office, ma'am."

Oh great, as if she wasn't nervous enough, they would both be in there. She crossed her fingers and stood tall. It was now or never. She walked to the office, her high heels clicking. She knocked on the door and BJ opened it. Jessie's pulse rose higher and her hands started to sweat. He had a sheepish look on his face.

"Come in and take a seat." He held the back of the chair for her and walked to the other side of the desk.

Jessie looked around the room. "Where's Bernard?" she whispered and leaned in closer.

"I'm Bernard." He rested his forearms on the desk and entwined his fingers. A lock of hair fell across his forehead.

"What?" Bernard was not a young man's name and from what she knew, he didn't own the place.

"I bought the garage from my dad a couple years ago." He watched her, as if waiting for her reaction before continuing.

"You're Bernard? Why didn't you tell me? You let me go on and on about how badly I wanted this job and you never said a word." She folded her arms across her chest, crossed her legs and swung her foot. Her chin jutted out and her eyes narrowed. How dare he deceive her? Was this some kind of sick joke he was playing?

"I truly had no idea who you were until you mentioned it at the ballgame. Then I didn't know what to do." He unclenched his hands and leaned back in the chair. "Don't take this the wrong way, but I didn't know if you were trying to scam me or just honestly trying to get a job. I like you and I was afraid of making the wrong decision for the wrong reason." BJ's gaze held hers. "I have too much time and too much money tied up in this project to lose everything because I had the hots for the sexiest woman this side of the Kanawha River."

BJ's shoulders sank, his hand fidgeting with a pencil. He looked like a boy that had been denied eating the last cookie but still had crumbs on his face. "You took me by surprise and I still haven't caught my breath."

Jessie's bad mood eased. It was hard to stay mad at a man saying all the right things. He looked remorseful, and the orgasms he'd given her still made her body blush. She just might forgive him after all—emphasis on the might.

"So what do we do now?" She raised an eyebrow and uncrossed her arms. It was best to hear what he had in mind before she made any rash decisions. She needed this job badly.

"Well, I did the same thing that I do for all applicants that I am thinking about hiring. I checked your references. I have a friend at Bauer's, a guy I went to school with. He told me I'd be a fool to not hire such a qualified employee to manage my business." BJ smiled and tapped his fingers on the desk.

"I know you wanted to be an investment partner, but I'm not ready to do that right now, if ever. We need to see how things go before even thinking about something like that. I hope you will consider staying even after your father's health improves." He continued to move the pencil back and forth across his fingers while he talked.

Jessie remained tightlipped as he talked. Was this a nervous habit? Being a salesperson was like being a poker player, you had to learn to read people. Know when to hold your cards and when to call their bluff. If you pushed too hard, they would send you out the door. She waited to see what he offered before making a plan of action. Just because they were good in bed didn't mean they would get along professionally.

"I've taken the liberty of writing up the job description, pay and benefits. If that is agreeable to you, you're hired." He handed her a paper with all the details.

Her eyes floated over the facts and figures, everything she had hoped for and more.

BJ twirled the pencil while she read, his eyes never leaving her face.

"I accept." Jessie smiled. It was a great deal. He either really liked her qualifications, really wanted her to stay, or a combination of both. Her heart returned to its resting beat. Her muscles began to relax. Things were definitely looking good. Jessie took a moment to daydream about having passionate sex in the stockroom with her handsome, younger boss. She grinned from ear to ear, happier than she'd been in ages.

"There is one more thing." BJ looked sullen. He rose and came around to the front and leaned that tight ass on the desk. Her cheeks flushed just thinking about how her hands had gripped the back of his thighs as he made love to her with a passion. "I had a fantastic weekend, Jessie. Actually, it was one of the best I can remember. Ever. Unfortunately, that part of our relationship ends now." He ran his hand through his hair before resting it on his hip. His chin was down, but his eyes looked up.

Over? "I'm afraid I don't know what you mean."

"The company has a policy set in place that prohibits dating amongst employees." His eyes never left hers. "It's to protect any female employees from being hit on and also save the company from any chance of sexual harassment lawsuits." BJ cleared his throat and straightened. "I've had it put in the training manual and contracts months ago when I was doing the business plan. I felt it was the right thing to do and I still do." BJ's voice cracked, the pencil stopped moving in his hands, and he placed it on the desk. "I never imagined that I'd meet a potential employee that I would actually want to get involved with."

Jessie had kept the calm expression on her face but her heart dropped. A lump settled in her throat and refused to move. How could she go from the elation of getting her dream job to the desperation of losing her dream guy in less than a few minutes' time? She couldn't breathe, her lungs on the verge of collapse.

What if he really hadn't wanted more than no-strings-attached-sex? Wasn't that what she wanted it to be? It was supposed to be a fun weekend with a younger man and some hot sex. It wasn't just hot, the earth had moved. But he couldn't see her cry, she had to be strong. Do the best she could. The smile froze on her face.

"Yes, of course, that would probably be for the best." She didn't believe a word that just left her mouth.

He stared intensely into her eyes. She squirmed in her chair and looked down to brush an imaginary piece of lint from her skirt. Her resolve returned, she sat up straight and looked him in the eye. How dare he just dismiss her like this? It should be her that broke off any future attachment and not her left feeling like she'd been dumped by the side of the road. How could she have been so easy to let go, without a fight? How could she win the job but lose the man? Not that she had him in the first place but still.

Well, they would see about that. Bernard Spencer had no idea who he was dealing with. She would be the best manager he ever had, and if it was meant to be, they'd be more than just business partners again soon. If she decided to stay that is, but with each minute she spent with the man, it would be harder and harder to go.

Jessie flashed him a grin and took a deep breath. His eyes zoomed to her raised breasts, and he licked his lips. A spark ignited within her. He did still want her, she could see it in his eyes and suddenly it felt like a competition, a battle of wills. Who would give in first? This was a challenge she would enjoy winning. In just a few months, he wouldn't be able to live without her or keep his hands off her. How she wanted those hands on her again...She could see the desire in his eyes and smell the spice of his cologne.

"So, do you want to see the place?" Mr. Spencer had an authoritarian tone to his voice. He rose, crossed to open the office door and waited for her response.

"Yes, I have today free." Jessie grabbed her purse and left the office in front of him. "I have to be on the road for a week and a half, but I'll give my two weeks' notice to my boss today." Despite the turn of events in their relationship, she couldn't wait to get started at her new job. It was time for a change and the new venture was exciting to say the least.

BJ stopped, addressing greasy-hand-man. "Tom, this is Jessie Knutson. She'll be the new assistant manager for the store. I'm going to show her the location. If you need anything, call my cell."

"Okay, boss. It's nice to meet you, ma'am." Tom waved the wrench in his hand and returned to the job.

"It's nice to meet you, too, Tom. Have a nice day," Jessie managed to say while hurrying to keep up with her new employer. He'd already opened the passenger side door to his truck. She threw her purse on the seat and lifted the hem of her skirt to climb in. When BJ touched her arm she flinched, a bolt of electricity jolting through her body.

He reeled back, his hands up like a bank teller during a stick-up. "Sorry, just trying to help you into the seat. I didn't know there would be voltage involved," he claimed with a grin.

"That's okay. I can manage." She lifted her skirt an inch or two higher. If he wasn't charged up now, he would be. Heavens to Bessie, her toes still twitched. Safely situated in the seat, she crossed her legs, exposing the skinny pair of thigh highs she'd donned for the interview. BJ leaned against the door, feasting his eyes on her legs. Now it was his turn to blush.

Giddiness filled her heart. How long would he last before he changed his work policy and pleaded for her to take him back? Not soon enough, an inner voice tweeted. She finally risked a glance in his direction. "Are you ready to go?"

"Yes, ma'am." She watched his Adam's apple bob.

He shut the door and walked head down to the other side of the truck. If she was reading his lips correctly, he'd liked what he just saw. BJ stopped at the other side of the truck and appeared to adjust his pants.

Jessie's mood lifted. She couldn't help but feel excited to start working on the initial steps of opening a new business. Her purse held a notebook of ideas and strategies she'd had for years. If only it was her business they were setting up and not someone else's but Jessie didn't have the funding to go it alone. Her admiration for BJ grew even higher. It was a big accomplishment for anyone let alone someone that was not yet thirty. The truck moved as BJ—make that Bernard—settled his large frame into the cab.

Why did things have to be complicated? His demeanor all business. Jessie resolved again to make this partnership work, in the office and in the bedroom. No way would he ever think about breaking off a relationship with her again. This man would be hers soon again and he would be the one to break first. Her fantasies would be fulfilled again soon. Before long, BJ would beg to have her take him back. He just didn't know it yet.

CHAPTER NINE

~ BJ ~

BJ SWORE HE'D BEEN HIT by a truck. The emotion-filled morning had his stomach in knots. Since he'd met Jessie, his life had been an up and down rollercoaster of sensations. Some blew his mind and some broke his heart. The look on her face when he explained they could only have a professional relationship still haunted him. Maybe she really did have feelings for him but yet she still took the job.

She had a smile on her face but he swore he saw her flinch. Damn, he felt like he had just kicked a puppy. He'd never do anything to hurt her, but it had to be done. To protect both of them.

Hell, he still remembered the mess his cousin, Jason, got in for dating one of the employees at his restaurant. Everything was all hot and heavy until she got jealous of a new waitress for no reason and then all hell broke loose. Even though they had lived together for months and nothing had happened with the new girl, that didn't stop her from going off the deep end and filing a sexual harassment lawsuit. His cousin barely kept his business after they settled out of court. BJ ran his fingers through his hair and gazed over at his passenger.

He couldn't afford to let his guard down or get his dick up. The smart thing would have been to not hire her, but he did need her. Her resume spoke volumes for all the experience she had. Jessie would be a welcome asset that any employer would kill to have. He just couldn't have her. It was the smart thing to do but not the easy thing to do. She had to be hands off, literally, even if it killed him.

BJ gazed at the passing landscape, roadside signs, the odometer, anything to keep his eyes away from those long legs of hers. Those same legs that just yesterday were wrapped around his waist as he pounded inside her. His brain wouldn't let IT rest. There had to be a way to have her in his life and in his bed. His cock jerked—at least that part of him thought it was a good idea. Maybe they could keep the two parts of their lives separate? Take things slow. Hell, no. BJ exhaled. He had to do the right thing.

BJ hit the turn signal and aimed the truck in the direction of Charleston. The extra cost of being just off the interstate was worth every penny. The free-standing building would be the first place anyone saw coming into Charleston from that direction. He parked the truck in front and walked to open the door for Jessie. The fear he might ignite kept him from touching her again. His eyes followed every curve, every movement as she slipped out of the cab. Her graceful hands smoothed her skirt and adjusted her shirt. Her face glowed.

"This is perfect! Location, location, location, as they say." Her arms outstretched as she circled and pointed at the road. "You need a huge billboard for the highway."

"I've already got one in the works," he tossed out while searching for the right key and heading for the entrance.

He unlocked and they entered the building, the lack of fixtures made it look huge.

"The shelves will be installed the end of the week. The front counter will be here." His hand indicated the different areas of placement as they toured the new facility. "Back here will be your office and mine will be across the hall." He followed her in. A smile was on her face. The room still needed furniture but it did have a nice view from the window.

"I love it. It's wonderful and I'm not just talking about the office. The whole floor plan is spot-on." She walked while talking and returned to stand in front of him. Her arms were crossed.

His chest swelled. He knew it looked good but it felt great to have someone second the opinion.

"Well, let's get started. We've got a lot of things to go over." BJ had her follow him to the office where he took a seat behind the desk. Yes, they had things to go over. It was going to be a long day as all he really wanted to do was bend her over the desk.

~ JESSIE ~

Jessie threw her purse on the bed. It was a nice room, very nice actually. Bauer's spared no expense when it came to her accommodations. No sleazy motel rooms for their employees. Unfortunately, all the grandeur of the room just made her feel worse. She placed her fast food bag on a table. Usually she loved the fast food crispy chicken Southwest salad, but today it held no appeal. After giving her two weeks' notice, she still had to finish all her contracted stops while also working for BJ. Jessie sighed as she ripped the top off the salad dressing packet.

She had so many things to be excited about. The challenges of helping start a business were a dream come true. Nevertheless, she'd never felt so lonely. The long list of tasks sat before her. All the employee applications were being sent to her. She had to narrow them down and start lining up interviews for when she returned to Charleston. The inventory supply list was almost completed and ready to email for BJ's approval. She chose a local computer specialist to work on the computers, website, and everything IT related. Her notebook held estimates for television, radio, and newspaper advertising. An apparel catalog earmarked her choices for the staff uniforms.

Jessie rested her jaw on a fist as she tasted the first forkful of crispy chicken. She lacked the ambition to even chew. Why hadn't he called? Sure, they had emailed several times a day but it was all business. No "how are you?" or "what's new?" or "I miss you so much I could die." Had their weekend together meant nothing to him? Was she expecting too much? Policy or no policy, she missed him.

Jessie pushed the salad away, her appetite gone. Maybe a hot bath would help. She kicked off her shoes and hit the remote. Applause from a game show echoed through the room as she walked to the bathroom. Adding some vanilla-scented bubble bath to the warm water made the huge tub look inviting. Her business clothes tossed to the floor, she dipped a pedicured toe in and tested the water.

It was perfect. Her weary body relaxed as she sank in up to her neck. The moist air cleared the headache threatening to throb in her brain. The whirlpool of water invigorated her spirit and stirred her imagination. She visualized BJ in the tub with her. His hands moving along her skin. Her half closed eyes glazed over just thinking about it

Her cell phone sang in the other room. Her eyes flashed open. Was it him? She couldn't move her heart pounding. The ring tone ended too quickly. Her heart sank. It was probably a wrong number. Jessie slid lower in the tub as a frown crossed her lips

The chimes from the other room rang out again.

"Dammit!" A frustrated Venus rose from the tub and water flowed down her glistening body. Her legs ached as she ran for the phone. "This had better be important," she spat at the ringing phone. Her hands shook as she saw BJ's number displayed on the screen. "Ah, hello?" She managed to say before the phone slid from her wet hand and a curse word left her mouth.

"Jessie. Jessie. Are you all right?" BJ's voice sounded from the phone on the floor.

She dried her hand and picked it up. "I'm here. Sorry, I was in the bath and I dropped the phone." Silence echoed between them. "Are you there?"

"Oh, Yes. Sorry. I…" He cleared his throat and continued. "I called to check on you. I mean, check on the progress you have been making with all the details. I know you must be swamped, so I wanted to see if there was anything I could help with."

"I've made great progress. Could you hold while I grab a towel? I'm dripping water all over the floor." She reached for a fluffy white hotel towel.

"Ah, sure." His voice deep.

Jessie swore he sounded…what? Turned on. A smile curved her lips. Maybe he missed her after all. Too bad they weren't on webcam. Oops, no more towel. Down girl, Jessie scolded, but couldn't help but feel inspired.

"There, all dried off and covered up." And dying for your touch. "Which reminds me, I was looking at uniform options. Bauer's was a stickler for no tattoos showing. Are you good with short sleeve shirts?"

"Hell yeah, with all mine, I'd be covered from head to toe so short sleeves are fine."

Her mind drifted to all the ink decorating his gorgeous body. What fun it would be to spend a lazy afternoon playfully filling in all the lines with an erasable marker.

"And stockings?" She'd hoped to plant a visual in his head as well.

"Ah, I'll leave that up to you."

"I think they won't be necessary. It will be khakis for everyone and skorts as another option for the women employees."

"I have no idea what those are but I'll take your word for it."

"Done. What details were you interested in discussing?" She returned to the table, her laptop and notebook waiting there.

"Well, I... Oh, yeah. How are we coming with the applicants?"

She didn't care about the applicants. She was coming just hearing his voice. She shook her head to clear her thoughts and focused on business. "There are several good ones that I definitely want to interview and a few maybes. I will email you the names and resumes of the ones I think might work. If they are agreeable to you, I will contact them and set up times to meet the week I get back."

"When will you be back?" His voice, a soft low whisper, sent chills running down her arm.

She crossed her legs and touched a pencil to her lips. The image of him running a pencil across his fingers came to mind.

"In about a week. Why? Have you missed me?" She bit her lip. If she could suck those words back in her mouth, she would. Why did she ask? He was her boss now, not the hottie from the garage. She'd overstepped her boundaries and now had to wait for the penalty call from bench.

There was no response.

She eyed the screen. The battery was fully charged. Had they been disconnected? A beep on the other line said they hadn't.

"I'm sorry, Jessie. I've been waiting all day for this call. It's the electricians for the sign. I'll talk to you again soon."

The line clicked before she had a chance to respond.

"Damn, damn, and double damn." She whipped the pencil across the room. "Why did I have to say something so stupid? Ugh!" The wet towel dropped to floor and she started to dress. To heck with the salad, this was an emergency. Grabbing her keys, she fled the room to look for the nearest ice cream store, chocolate shop, or liquor store whichever one she saw first.

CHAPTER TEN

~ BJ ~

BJ COUNTED HIS BLESSINGS. THANK goodness for bad timing, although the electrician probably thought he was a blubbering idiot. The last things he wanted to talk about were exit signs and computer outlets. "Do what you think," was his response to every question. He'd be paying a big bill for that lack of attention to detail.

How could he think of specifics when he couldn't get the image of a wet and naked Jessie out of his mind? He had an instant hard-on the second she answered the phone. Did he miss her? Hell, yeah. She was all he could think about and the reason he had to get off the phone before making a fool of himself.

Where was she, what was she doing, what was she wearing or not wearing and how soon could he see her again? Jessie was a distraction he just couldn't afford right now.

Even Buddy had been moping around since she'd left. He would sit on the deck, not wanting to come in at night. BJ didn't want to come in at night either. The place seemed empty. Call him a slob but he'd not had the heart to wash the sheets since that weekend. At least he could hug her pillow and enjoy the scent of her perfume left behind. Why didn't he have the balls to tell her he missed her?

He sat back in the desk chair and crossed an ankle over his knee. BJ gazed out the office window. Every night since she'd left, he'd entered her number on the phone. A finger poised above the call button that he never hit, until tonight. How was this even going to work out? If he had been able to control the animal lust he'd felt for her that stormy day in the garage, none of this would be an issue now. A smile crossed his lips. It'd been worth it and was a memory he could never regret.

~ *JESSIE* ~

J ESSIE PUNCHED HER PILLOW AND rolled onto her back.

She'd tossed and turned all night and the phone never rang again. The back of her hand rested on her forehead and the other was flung to the side of the bed. Why were things such a mess? She rolled to her side. The blank wall of the hotel room was holding no answers. It was time to go to work. She had a job to do and it would be done to the best of her abilities. Even if BJ didn't want her, she would make sure she didn't fail him. Rising from the bed, Jessie opened her laptop. In no time at all the ideas were clicking. Her business suggestions were outlined and sent to BJ's email. She finished dressing and gave the room one last look before heading out the door. It would be all business from now on. Her dad needed her and that's all that mattered.

Jessie wrestled with the keys to her Charleston apartment while balancing flowers and a box filled with going away presents. At least she would finally get to spend some time here as it was just a short drive to BJ's new store. Heck, she might even buy a house plant.

The week had passed quickly. Jessie had thrown herself into work and even surpassed her sales record for the month. It felt good to end her time with Bauer's on a high note. A surprise farewell party had awaited her as she made her last stop at her employer's. She would miss her coworkers and several offered to take her out for drinks at closing time. She declined with the excuse of having other plans.

Some plans, she scoffed—laundry, buying groceries, and doing the finishing touches on her interview questions for applicants on Monday. She was exhausted and if she sat down, she'd probably collapse. A six pack of the same beer they'd shared sat on the kitchen counter. BJ's handsome face floated across her mind. He hadn't called again but emailed daily.

She kicked off her shoes and traded business wear for comfort. Grey shorts, flip flops, and her

West Virginia Express shirt, the one that BJ had given her. Returning to her car, she grabbed some grocery bags out of the trunk.

"Need some help with that?" The deep Southern drawl raised goose bumps along her back. Bent over the bags in her trunk, her heart skipped a beat as she caught a glimpse of tanned, well-muscled legs behind her. BJ, here, in her driveway!

"Yeah, that would be nice." Her trembling arms offered him a bag. "Thanks." He looked good, damn good. A sexy, five o'clock shadow graced his strong jaw. His hair looked tousled and brushed his forehead. A pair of shorts slung low on his hips and Jessie's breath caught. He was wearing the same grey T-shirt she'd worn that morning at his house. Was that deliberate?

"What brings you to this neighborhood?" Her voice shook. Her heart pounded so loud he could probably hear it. She twisted to grab another bag and shut the trunk. "And how did you know where I live?"

"Job application." He smiled. "I needed to talk to you and I didn't want it to be on the phone."

Jessie started toward her apartment, leaving BJ to follow. "Oh, yeah? Business or pleasure?" Jessie clamped her mouth shut. He was her boss. She had to stop with the flirting.

"A little of both."

She risked a look in his direction but couldn't read his face. His eyes spoke volumes, though. He did want her. She licked her lips, swallowed, and crossed the threshold of the apartment door.

"You can just set those on the table. I better put some of these things in the fridge before they spoil. Could you hand me the milk?" Her hand reached out.

"Sure, let me help." BJ chose some other refrigerated items from the bag. His fingers grazed Jessie's and her nipples puckered as if he had touched them. Her cheeks blushed and her ears were aflame. Chills ran down her legs, and it wasn't from the cold air of the refrigerator.

"Where do you want these?" BJ held a cereal box in each hand.

"In the cupboard above would be great." She indicated the correct cabinet as she bent to pick up a plastic bag that fluttered to the floor.

Rising, her eyes locked on the two masculine hands that came to rest on the countertop, one on each side of her.

"You smell wonderful," he whispered and his breath tickled the back of her neck. A stubbly chin tickled her ear. BJ's strong arms wrapped her in a tender embrace. "I can't seem to get you out of my mind."

She inhaled a whiff of pine cologne. Jessie clutched the counter with quaking hands. Without thinking, she leaned back in his arms and a moan escaped her lips. He held her tight, his arousal warm and throbbing on her lower back. Her breasts ached, eager and ready for his touch. The pleasure of being in his arms again was overwhelming. Turning, she tried to read the look in his dark, brown eyes. Desire, yes.

The countertop pressed into her back as he leaned in. Her breasts heaved and pressed into his chest. Sexual tension filled the room with heavy breathing the only sound. She pulled his pelvis tight to hers, the anticipation of making love again stimulating her no end. BJ unraveled the scrunchy from her hair, letting it tumble free to her shoulders as he tossed it aside. His fingers threaded in her locks as his lips inched closer. Jessie's heart pounded so loud she could hear it. He stopped, his eyes questioning.

"Jessie, open the door, we know you're in there." Loud voices and heavy knocking rattled the door. What the hell?

"Were you expecting company?" BJ rested his forehead on hers.

"No. I better go see what is going on." An aggravated groan exploded from her lips as she marched to the pounding on the front door. She flung it open.

"Surprise!" A crowd of former coworkers hollered.

"You didn't think we would let you leave without a party, did you?" her former manager asked.

Jessie stood speechless. An imaginary bucket of cold water thrown on her body still pulsating from BJ's touch.

"Oh, wow. You guys didn't need to do that." She wanted to sound excited but it didn't come out that way. The voice in her head repeated the sentence complete with a few swear words added. She smoothed back her hair and straightened her shirt.

"The rest of the group is waiting at the bar down the street. No need to grab your purse, drinks are on us." All eyes looked behind her. She followed their gaze to BJ leaning against the kitchen doorway. His shirt now hung loose, hiding his desire.

"Uh, sorry, we didn't know you had a visitor."

Jessie had told them she had plans. Unfortunately, everyone knew about her lack of a social life and didn't believe her. Her gaze fell to inspect the floor while hoping some answer was written there.

"Hey, that sounds great." BJ draped a possessive arm across her shoulder. "You have to have a farewell party. Drinks would be great, wouldn't they, Jessie?"

"Sure. Let me grab my keys and we'll meet you there." She half-smiled and waved them on. The group backed off her doorstep and headed for the bar. Some called back to remind her not to be late as she shut the door.

"We don't have to go, you know." She frowned while stuffing her keys in a pocket.

"Yeah, we do. They're your friends and you'll regret not going if you don't. I'm sorry. I shouldn't have come on to you like that. We have a lot of things to talk about." He watched out the window. "We shouldn't have . . . we should probably meet in public from now on." Her heart sank. "But the truth is I can't control myself around you. You light me on fire like no woman ever has." He twisted in her direction. "I want to do right by you, Jessie. I'm your boss but I wish I wasn't." He walked over and dropped a light kiss on her forehead. "I'll wait outside for you."

What the hell just happened? Jessie took a drink of water and put the scrunchy back in her hair. She was determined to win him back no matter what it took. Her heart couldn't take much more of the hot and cold treatment.

CHAPTER ELEVEN

~ BJ ~

A ROWDY BUNCH GREETED THEM AS they entered the front door of the bar. They looked like a couple wearing their matching baseball team shirts. BJ knew some of the guys so he fit in just fine. Jessie appeared to be having a good time laughing and drinking with the people who had been her coworkers. He couldn't help but stare at her. She shone like a bright light. The gorgeous red hair hard to miss. He grabbed a seat next to Brad Johnson, the guy that gave Jessie the glowing job reference.

"So, what's up with you and Jessie?" Brad motioned with his beer bottle and took a drink.

"What do you mean?" BJ signaled to the waitress for another round.

"You know damn well what I mean. We interrupted something and I don't think you were there helping to hang curtains."

BJ continued to stare at Jessie.

"The guys and I think of her as a member of the family. You hurt her and we'll beat the shit out of you."

BJ shook off the threat. "I have no intention of hurting her." He took a swig of his beer, setting it down harder than he intended.

"Well, something has been bothering her for the last two weeks. She's been moping around like she lost her best friend. I know you're a few years younger than her, but don't make the mistake of thinking this is some kind of game." Brad's finger poked him in the chest. "Jessie's a class act and don't forget it."

"I don't and I won't. I hired her, didn't I? I have no intention of compromising one of my employees."

"Good, but I get the feeling that you think of her as more than an employee so spill."

"Fine. We hooked up before I knew she wanted the job."

"So?" Brad raised his glass to his lips.

"So? How do I know she didn't sleep with me in the hopes of getting me to hire her?" BJ couldn't shake the memory of being used before. His heart knew Jessie wasn't like that, but his head kept shedding doubt.

"You saw her resume. You'd have hired her anyway, and like I said Jessie is a class act. I don't ever recall her having a casual hook up. That I heard of anyway. Sure she dated now and then but it was never serious. When you're on the road, relationships are hard to maintain."

"That's the other thing. I don't even know why I hired someone that doesn't want to stay in one place. She even admitted that she only came home to take care of her dad until he's better."

"We all grow up, BJ. We all eventually want to put down roots. Jessie's dad is fine. He's just getting older, like we all are. If you ask me, I think she wanted an excuse to stay here."

"You really think so?" BJ scratched his chin.

"I know so."

After the lecture from Brad, the conversation returned to baseball, fishing, and former classmates. BJ was getting a headache. Coming here was a mistake but he didn't want Jessie to miss out on spending time with her friends. They obviously cared about her a lot. Jessie was always in his eyesight. Her bright smile lit up the room. He couldn't help but glare whenever a male coworker approached to hug her goodbye. BJ made sure to keep an eye out for any overaggressive hands, but everyone treated her with love and respect.

As the evening progressed, everyone bought her drinks. Jessie returned from the bathroom and BJ could see her step looked a little shaky. He leisurely rose from his stool and walked to her side.

"How are you doing?" He had to speak loudly in her ear over the blaring jukebox.

"Great," she yelled, spinning so fast he had to reach out to steady her.

"Whoa, I think we better get you home while you can still walk."

Jessie threw her arms around him. "You're so sweet. Are you going to tuck me in bed, too?" She trailed a fingertip along his jaw.

BJ could feel Brad's eyes scorching his back.

"Whatever it takes to get you out of here, grab your stuff and let's go." She was going to have one hell of a hangover if he didn't get her out of the place soon. It was probably too late for that as it was.

They left the bar and walked in silence. Their fingers bumped a few times before he grasped her small hand in his. Hand-in-hand they walked down the sidewalk. So much for acting like her boss, but he didn't care. BJ made it known to any men giving her the eye that she was taken, even if it was just for the walk home.

"It was a fun night. I'm going to miss those guys," Jessie finally said.

"Yes, they obviously think very highly of you. I'm sure the feeling is mutual." The cold night air was a welcoming relief to the fervor that he felt whenever she was near.

Within moments they returned to her apartment. Jessie fumbled with the keys before opening the door. He hesitated. It was a mistake to be alone with her, but his feet moved of their own free will, obviously not listening to any commands coming from his head. He glanced at her gorgeous ass and his body hummed. Damn he wanted her and wanted her bad. He followed her inside to the kitchen like a puppy dog begging for a treat. He'd take any handout she gave him.

BJ braced a hand on the kitchen chair, watching her as she staggered to the couch and lay down. He closed his eyes in a half prayer. Give me strength. His grip on the chair tightened, his knuckles white.

Again, the traitorous limbs led him to kneel by her side.

Hot pink polish accented her tan slender toes. His gaze floated to trim ankles that had once crossed behind his back. A moan escaped his lips remembering that moment too long ago when her shapely legs were entwined around him. Breathing labored, BJ traced his fingers where his eyes had just been, starting with those delicate feet. They traveled over the slender bones of her ankle, around the bend of her knee and glided upward along her thigh.

He dropped to his knees. BJ cupped her ass cheek and squeezed, his balls tightening. Jessie purred and rolled toward him. She grasped his other hand and pulled it toward her chest. His hand regretfully left her ass and skimmed the length of her back before tangling in her silky red hair. He breathed deeply. It may be wrong but damn it felt right. He yearned to kiss her until she begged him to make love to her. Her pouty lips parted as if reading his mind—and a slight snore escaped. What the fuck? Her eyes were shut.

"Jessie?" He gave her a gentle nudge. No response. "Are you asleep?"

"I'm so tired," Jessie mumbled, shifting and rolling over. The light, alcohol-induced snore continued.

BJ laughed and sat back on his heels.

"Son of a—" He ran shaking fingers through his hair. Nothing was going to happen tonight. "Well, I guess that decides that." He covered Jessie with a nearby blanket and dropped a lingering kiss on her forehead. BJ couldn't leave just yet so he watched her sleep, afraid she might wake up and become sick. Being in the same room with her was a comfort he wasn't ready to relinquish. He spent the next few hours reading some newspapers and studying an auto supply catalogue that'd been lying on the kitchen table. When the clock hit two, he remembered Buddy. He had to get home. His lips touched her hair one last time.

They had a business to open and the next few weeks would be hectic to say the least. "Sleep well, beautiful." Someday, darling, you'll be mine again and it won't be just for a weekend.

CHAPTER TWELVE

~ *JESSIE* ~

THE LEAVES OF THE TREES danced in the wind outside her office window. Jessie rested her chin on her hand. What had happened when they returned from her going away party a month ago? The night was still a blur. As soon as her head hit the couch pillow, she was out. When she woke up the next morning, she was covered in a blanket, a glass of water and a bottle of aspirin sitting nearby. Since then, her words with BJ had been brief and usually in the form of an email.

She hadn't seen him much except for the day they opened the doors for the first time two weeks ago. It seemed like they were just passing each other coming and going. As the assistant manager, there was no need for her to be there at the same time he was working. Now that the place was up and going, isolation set in. When she had a day off, there was always an appointment to take her dad to or something she had to do around home. Alone at night she had too much time on her hands and not much on her mind, except BJ, that was.

Jessie gave herself the once-over in the full-length mirror attached to the back of her office door. Today was a big day. The chamber of commerce ribbon cutting was at two. Everyone would be there, but the only one she cared about was BJ. Her heart hurt. Her body ached. She adjusted the tie on the front of her black silk blouse and smoothed a wrinkle from the beige skirt.

She looked at the clock—nine forty-five. Her palms began to sweat. She would see him soon. Why did he still have to affect her this way? She hated that he could still make her nervous as a schoolgirl and just the sight of him sent butterflies fluttering to her stomach. Jessie inhaled a deep breath and proceeded out the door and right into BJ.

"Oops." Her hands crushed to his chest as he reached to steady her.

"Sorry, didn't mean to scare you. I was coming to get you. You have to be in the picture." Jessie looked in his eyes and found herself at a loss for words.

"Cat got your tongue, Jessie?" He grinned and stepped back.

"Ah, yes, I've never seen you in a suit before. You clean up good, BJ." *Good?* He was cover model good. She licked her lips. Her hands trembled as a vision of him without the suit flashed before her eyes.

"I have to look good for the bigwigs." He straightened his tie and winked. "The newspaper will be taking some photos, too. Are you ready to go?" BJ offered his arm.

"Pictures. Yeah. Right." Her brain still set on pause. It'd been all business for the last two weeks and now he decided to be Prince Charming. BJ was obviously playing for the cameras. She calmed her heart to a normal rate. It was all for show probably. No need to get the blood pressure up. Her hand rested in the crook of his arm like it belonged there, a quiet moment of calm before the storm.

"Can I escort you out before I have to meet with the press?"

"Sure." Anything to be close to the man she couldn't stop thinking about.

Total chaos reigned as they entered the front of the store and the place jumped with excitement. BJ squeezed her fingers and let go of her arm to shake hands with local dignitaries.

Her eyes took in the details to make sure everything was in place. The caterers had put the final touches on the refreshment table and a large door prize box sat nearby. Although they had been open for two weeks, it had just been a soft opening with no advertising. BJ had wanted to get the staff used to all the operations of the business without having to deal with large crowds. Today the place was packed for their official grand opening.

A group of people in business attire walked through the door, a photographer from the Daily Mail trailing behind. Jessie couldn't help but feel proud of BJ and all he'd accomplished. Yes, she'd had a big hand in it, but she wouldn't be here if it wasn't for him. Jessie watched as he shook hands with the group and directed them her way.

"Gentlemen, I would like to introduce you to Miss Jessie Knutson. I couldn't have opened this place without her." BJ motioned her way.

Jessie blushed as the group acknowledged her. Each man introduced himself and offered her their hand.

"Let's get a photo of the two of you in front of the sign," the photographer suggested and led them to the front door.

The flashbulbs flared. The questions never stopped. The reporters wanted her advice on everything from how to start a business to what kind of battery to buy. Her ego expanded with all the attention. The day would have been perfect except for the fact that every time she turned around Kayla—her younger blonde replacement from Bauer's—seemed to be glued to BJ's side.

As a favor to Bauer's, they'd agreed to intern Kayla for a couple of months so she could learn about things from the ground up. It was a good idea, not everyone had the background Jessie had when she got hired.

Kayla was qualified and just doing her job. What bugged Jessie was how young the woman was. That and the matter of her hanging around BJ like a lovesick teenager. Truthfully, Kayla was probably farther away in age than she and BJ were, but still. There would always be acceptance of older men with younger women.

Heck, what was she thinking, setting her eyes on a younger man who could get any chick he wanted and probably did? Her heart split in half and her hands shook. She'd wasted her time thinking he was going to want a relationship with her. What a fool she had been. Jessie'd accomplished her dream of managing a shop, but at what cost? She'd won the battle but lost the war.

The rest of the day was a blur. The grand opening had gone well and pretty much everything had been put away and cleaned up. Jessie took a moment to lean against the wall and collect her thoughts.

"Why the frown?" A deep voice disturbed her peace.

Jessie jumped and nearly spilled the cup of punch in her hand. Her other hand rose to press against her beating heart.

"Sorry. I didn't mean to scare you." BJ now stood in front of her.

"I wasn't frowning. Just deep in thought." And thinking about the handsome guy next to her. Maybe working together wasn't such a good idea. His spicy aftershave encouraged her to lean closer.

"Well, you should be celebrating a job well done. I can't believe how smoothly everything went." His smile was bright and it was hard to look away.

"It did go well, didn't it?" The place looked fantastic. They made a great team.

"Thanks to you." BJ held a bouquet of wildflowers. "These are for you."

Jessie shook her head to clear the cobwebs. "You're giving me flowers?"

"Not just me. They're from everyone." He handed them her way while he waved his hand at the group that had gathered around. Their employees applauded as her cheeks turned crimson. She'd gone from a high of thinking he'd bought her flowers to a low of finding out they were from the whole crew.

Jessie scolded herself for feeling so selfish. This was a really sweet gesture and from the looks on everyone's faces, well except for maybe Kayla's, they really meant the kindness behind it. She set her glass on a shelf and held the blooms to her nose.

"I love them and can't thank you enough." The smell was amazing. A combination of every sweet scent you would experience outdoors. She always loved wildflowers over roses and couldn't wait to put these by her nightstand. "Whoever picked them out did a wonderful job. These are perfect."

A few people pointed to BJ. He tucked his fingers in his pockets and glanced at the ground. Actually, anywhere but her. A grin teased her mouth. This wasn't just a bouquet that you picked off the shelf. Yes, it was from a flower shop but anyone could see there had been thought put into it.

When they'd been out fishing, she'd pointed out flowers along the shore. Jessie had always loved the yellow, blue, and purple colors but she had mentioned that sunflowers were her favorite. Funny thing, the flowers were from everyone but it felt like they were really from him.

Jessie would have appreciated anything they'd given but she loved this arrangement because it was picked with her in mind. It had to have been.

The bouquet was filled with yellow, blue, and purple wildflowers with sunflowers taking the center.

After the crowd dispersed, BJ was still by her side. By the look on his face, he knew he'd been caught putting more thought into the gift than a boss should.

"Thank you, BJ." She briefly touched her hand to his arm. The heat from his skin could be felt through his dress shirt. The urge to wrap her arms around him, had her clutching the flowers tighter to her chest."

"Like I said, they were from everyone."

"Yes, and everyone knew I adored sunflowers." She lifted an eyebrow and smirked.

"Well, I wanted to make sure you liked them." He pulled at the collar of his shirt.

"I don't like them," she teased. "I love them."

"I'm glad." He gave her that smile that always made her heart leap. "You deserve them."

An awkward pause followed as they watched the crew getting ready to close up.

"I've something coming up next weekend that I was wondering if you would like to go to."

"What is it?" She held her breath.

"It's a charity event to raise money for the veterans' home. The shop is a sponsor and I thought you might like to attend."

"Of course. What can I do to help?" Anything that involved helping veterans, she would gladly do.

"Nothing really. It's a ride and then picnic at the bar just outside town." He mentioned the name and she knew exactly which one it was. It was a well-known biker bar.

"You have a bike?" How had she missed that?

"Of course, every good southern boy has one." The light in his eyes sparkled again. Here was the flirty man she craved.

"Not *every* southern boy," now it was her turn to flirt, "only the really good ones." Her gaze floated from his lips to his eyes.

"Is that so?" BJ stepped closer but not as close as she'd like.

"Yes. I'll go." Her whole day just got better.

"Great. I'll pick you up Saturday morning around eight, if you don't mind riding with me on the run."

"Can I wear leather?" Jessie purred. If that didn't get his engine running nothing would. Right now, she didn't care if this went beyond mutual respect in the workplace, she was dying for his touch.

"Honey, you can wear anything you want." His voice was husky and low. "Maybe this one time, on Saturday we won't have to be just business associates." He shrugged his shoulders. "We can just enjoy the day together, right?"

"Absolutely." Jessie turned and walked back to her office. Her step was lighter and so were her hopes. For as long as she was in town, Jessie wanted BJ in her life.

CHAPTER THIRTEEN

~ BJ ~

IT WAS A STUPID GAME they were playing. One that never should have been started but there was no way he could quit now.

Jessie was all he could think about when he wasn't working his ass off at both places. He thought the garage could run smoothly without him there but it was always something. His father even mentioned coming back from Florida to help out but that wouldn't be right. The guy had retired and was thoroughly enjoying his life there. Unfortunately, BJ couldn't be in two places at once. It wasn't in him to close up the shop either.

The garage had been in that community forever. People desperately needed the services they provided there. Bernard's was the only full-service garage for miles around. It was quite a drive and a lot of expense if you had to tow a vehicle that long of a distance.

Just thinking about Jessie out there by herself with a flat tire on that barren stretch of road could have ended very badly. Not just money-wise but what if he hadn't come along when he did. And with a severe storm about to hit.

Jessie was a smart woman. She could take care of herself but bad things happened to good people every day. It just wouldn't be right to close the garage and leave the local people with no one to service. But finding someone he could trust and was competent enough to make decisions in his absence was proving to be a problem.

It was fine when he was at the garage, and he could even leave it for a day or two but weeks at a time was causing a lot of concern. Even today a sense of guilt crawled down his spine. Saturdays were always busy with last minute things to get done for those who worked during the week, but the Veterans ride was too important to miss. It was an important cause and the thought of having Jessie's arms around him on the bike was something he just couldn't pass up.

He'd been a wreck the last few weeks. Although there'd been a shit ton of stress with the opening, it could've been a lot worse if Jessie hadn't been by his side. BJ revved the gas on his motorcycle. That was also the problem. He wanted her by his side all the time and not just at work.

The bike ride had been a good idea to see if things between the two were really meant to be or if it was just the excitement of their weekend together that still had his heart in knots.

Pulling up to the door of her place, his jaw just about dropped to the ground. He'd recognize that hair anywhere but the rest of her was 'holy shit out of this world'.

Used to seeing her dressed in business attire, the motorcycle get-up was a jolt to his system. A shock that had him rethinking being such a dumbass about his no dating policy. Right now, he'd risk everything he had to be with her.

Jessie stepped out to greet him as he pulled the bike next to the curb. Turning off the engine, he sat back in the seat and whistled as she turned around.

"What do you think? Do I look like a biker?"

She wore a pair of skintight leather pants, tucked into biker boots, a leather vest, and what appeared to be a lace bra or top underneath. Damn. This was one fine woman.

"No, you look like a biker's lady. So get on the back and I'll take you for a ride." BJ handed her the extra helmet he'd brought.

Jessie put her hands on her hips. "Does that mean I'm yours?"

In his head he replied hell yeah, you're mine, but to be safe he said. "Let's just enjoy the day together and see where it goes, how about that?"

She pulled her hair back with a bandana and put on the helmet he offered. "Deal." Jessie laughed.

"Not before you put this on also." He tossed her a leather jacket. "It's a little big but if anything were to happen, better to be safe than sorry." Her ivory skin would burn in no time at all in the bright sun today.

She donned the coat and settled onto the back of his bike. Her arms slipped around his waist and BJ swore he sat a little taller. Jessie did that to him. They worked hard together and today they would play hard together. He covered her hand with his and squeezed it once.

"Let's ride, big guy." Excitement was in her voice.

"Your wish is my command." BJ turned the key and they were off.

They met up with the rest of the riders around ten. There was a backroad they would be taking before finally ending at the park.

The twists and turns of the hills and valleys around West Virginia made it an excellent route to take. He'd ridden this route many times but never had he enjoyed it as much as today. It was because of the woman with him.

Spending too much of his life working had brought him many successes but what did it really mean if you had no one to share it with you? He was ready to take a chance on love again.

Jessie was everything that he would look for in a woman, he'd just not known it until now. Smart, beautiful, sassy, and kind. Jessie was a natural at whatever she set out to do. As soon as they ended the ride, she was the first one off their bike, asking what she could do to help.

Jessie served food while he helped out with raffle tickets. He'd offered to switch places but she insisted that was where she wanted to be. Every time he looked in her direction, the woman was smiling and making new friends. Knowing her, Jessie was probably drumming up business for the store as well. BJ swore he saw her slip a few people her card.

"Who's your lady friend?" Charlie, one of the

other volunteers, took a seat next to him. The smell of chicken from his plate caused his stomach to growl.

"A co-worker."

"You're kidding me, right?" Charlie laughed and shoved a fork of potato salad into his mouth.

"No."

"Well then you won't mind if I ask her out?"

"Yeah, I would mind," he blurted out.

"Ha, I guess she isn't just a coworker now is she?" He dabbed at his chin with a paper napkin.

"Honestly, I don't know where we stand." BJ crossed his arms in front of his chest as he watched several guys talking to Jessie.

"Well, if I were you, I'd get off my ass and figure that out before someone else does."

"It's complicated." Boy was it ever. They had a weekend of hot sex and great fun and then he went and fucked everything up with a no dating clause. Still, at the time he didn't know if he could trust her. Jessie wasn't Ashton and he needed to stop thinking that every woman he met was only interested in him for his money or looking for a place to stay.

"Not really." Charlie interrupted his thoughts.

"Huh?" BJ's gaze settled on the woman that consumed his mind.

"It's simple. You either like her or you don't."

The man had a point. If only it was that easy.

"Which is it?" Charlie wasn't letting him off the hook.

BJ tapped his index finger on the wooden picnic

table. "I like her." That part he did know.

"Then I suggest you go stake a claim before someone else does."

It wasn't hard to miss all the guys returning to her table. BJ rolled his eyes. No one was that hungry, yet everyone kept coming back for more.

Son of a bitch. He couldn't leave his bench at the silent auction. It was important to sell tickets for the prizes and raise all they could for the charity.

"I got things under control." Charlie got up and tossed his now empty plate in a nearby trash can. He placed a hand on BJ's shoulder. "Why don't you take a break? Get something to eat."

"Don't mind if I do." He stood and headed for the food tables. His stomach growled but it was his heart that drew him to the lunch line.

Just the smile on her face when their eyes met, had him feeling ten pounds lighter.

"Hey there." Jessie handed him a plate. "I was wondering when you were going to get in line."

"I was waiting for a break. Seems to be a hungry group."

"Well, look at this spread. Everyone went all out." Her eyes were bright and her cheeks were pink. "I'm so glad you invited me. I'm having the best time today."

Of all the things she could say, this was what he least expected. "Really? I bring you here to work and you're having a good time."

"Why wouldn't I be?" Using a pair of tongs, Jessie placed a piece of chicken on his plate. "It felt great being on a bike again and I've met so many wonderful people here today. Not to mention we are raising a lot of money for a great cause."

It took all his strength not to go around the table and give her a huge hug and a kiss. Jessie was a kind and caring person as was everyone here, but to him she was starting to be so much more.

"Do you want another piece?"

"Huh?" BJ had been too busy staring at her beautiful face, that he didn't realize he was holding up the line. "Oh, no thanks. One is fine." He paused. "Say can you take a break and eat with me?" Jessie turned to the person in charge and got a thumbs up.

"Yeah, sure. You pick a spot and I'll meet you there."

It was at least ten minutes before she could join him at a table he'd found farthest from the crowd.

"Thanks again for bringing me today."

"I'm glad you enjoyed it. Not everyone is so excited about having to work on their day off."

"This isn't work." Jessie grinned. "But I have sent some business your way."

"I knew it," he teased. "Always on the clock, Knutson.

"Hey, I'm just trying to help people out."

"I know, but I invited you here today to have fun, not work."

"Work *is* fun to me," she confessed.

"Work is never fun." Who was he to talk, he'd been punching the clock since he was a kid.

"But yet we both are workaholics."

"It would seem so." They were just alike. Both

driven and successful. What a team they would make in the bedroom and the boardroom.

"You'll have a hard time replacing me." Jessie cracked open a beer and took a drink.

"Wait." He almost choked on his chicken. "What? Replace you?"

"Well, you know I came back here to help my dad."

"Yeah." It was hotter than hell out but he suddenly felt a chill.

"He's improving a lot. Faster than anyone had expected."

"That's good. Isn't it?"

"Yes, but it was never my plan to stay long term." Jessie bit her lip.

"What?" A knot just formed in his gut. "You took a job only intending to stay a few months?"

"Well, not really but you knew it was always my intent to only stay until he was better."

"Are you kidding me?" It was a toss-up as to whether or not he felt angry or betrayed. That she could leave him so easily kicked him in the heart. That she took the job of someone else that might want to stay permanently kicked him in the head. He knew she had told him this but still he never really believed her or wanted to believe her. "You loved your job at Bauer's. What were you planning to do? Get your old job back? And what about the store?" Now anger and shock set in. Had their passionate weekend together meant nothing at all?

"Look," she placed her hand on his forearm, "I don't know when I will leave. It all depends on my dad. I'm certainly not going away soon."

"But you still intend to leave?"

Jessie put her hands on her lap and shrugged. "I'm a wanderer. I don't know what will make me want to stay in one place."

"But what if we were dating? Would you just up and leave me?" This was messed up. How did he not see this coming? She was a traveling salesperson. Had been a traveling salesperson.

"Well, you made that not an option so it doesn't really matter does it?" Her eyes meet his and he had no answer for her. He'd made the stupid rule but in the brief time he'd known this woman he knew one thing for sure. Jessie was a rule breaker and it was breaking his heart not being with her. It wasn't Jessie's fault, it was his. But he didn't want her just for the time she was here, that wasn't an option. He wanted time. Time to see where their relationship could go.

Just getting rid of the policy wouldn't work. It was a good guideline to have, especially today. But he couldn't just sit by and watch the most intriguing, beautiful, and smart woman he'd ever met just walk out of this life.

If he had anything to do with it, he'd figure a way to make her stay.

CHAPTER FOURTEEN

~ JESSIE ~

PARKING HER CAR IN THE shade, Jessie strolled through the restaurant's lot to the front door. She wanted to pick up her father for lunch but he insisted he'd meet her there. Jessie muffled a yawn with her hand. After they had everything put away, BJ drove her home. They spent another hour standing by his bike, not wanting the night to end but it had to. Talking about anything and nothing just to extend the time together.

They were at a standstill right now. BJ admitted to wanting a relationship but it wasn't meant to be if she wasn't going to stay. Or could she?

Spying her father out on the deck, she waved and weaved her way around the many customers and their tables.

"Hi dad." She kissed her father on the cheek and took a seat across the table from him.

"Hey, sweetheart." Sparky Knutson smiled at his daughter. He was dressed in a t-shirt and shorts. A pair of sneakers on his feet. The guy had lost a few pounds but he'd been heavier than he should be. Her father had never met a donut he didn't like.

"You look great." His color was good. She'd missed most of his physical therapy after the heart attack but he'd thankfully made a speedy recovery. In fact, he looked better than he had in years. The strict diet and exercise program they had him on had done wonders. "Fantastic actually."

"Well, your brother's a slave driver. He has me out walking at the crack of dawn every day." Her father took a drink from the glass of water the waitress had just set in front of him. "I've gone through so much tread, I'll need another pair of shoes by the end of the week." He chuckled.

"I can take you." Jessie volunteered and Sparky rolled his eyes. "Where do you like to shop?" It stopped her short that she had no idea.

"How many times do I have to tell you kids that I'm fine? I appreciate everything but I'm not an invalid. I'm perfectly capable of going shopping by myself." He picked up the menu and continued to talk. "The doctor said I have no restrictions and to just keep up with the exercise and eating healthy."

"But. . ." She needed to do something to help. Travis had pretty much taken over but that was typical of him.

"No buts, dear. Just seeing your pretty face is all I need to feel better." He winked and studied the selection again.

Jessie groaned and tossed up her hands. She was almost relieved that the waitress drew their attention away from that discussion to place their order. Handing the woman their menus, the two locked eyes again.

"I guess there's no need for me to stay here then, is there?" Her lower lip quivered. So much for a future at Bernard's store. She insisted the new employees call him that, instead of BJ, and sometimes it still stuck in her head. "Hopefully they will hire me back at Bauer's." It was doubtful as they had replaced her but she'd try. What other options did she have?

"Of course, there is." Her father waved her comment away. "What are you talking about? It's about time you came home. Dammit girl. I miss you, Jess."

"But…" As much as she tried to fight it, she missed him and her brothers. Way too much.

"But what, dear?" Her father wasn't letting it go.

"Mom." It almost felt like a sore spot bringing the subject up. They seldom talked about her after her death. It was a pain so deep that nothing would pierce it.

"Mom, what?" Again, he held out his hands as if waiting for the answer to fall from the sky.

Did he not know? "She never wanted to stay here. You know that. All mom ever talked about was how she wanted to travel and see the world. But that never happened because she fell in love, got married, and before long, she was stuck here, in a place she didn't like."

"Because your mother didn't like it here, you don't either?" He frowned and it broke her heart. "But this is your home. It always has been and it always will be."

"I know and I have to admit, it's been really nice being back. I actually have a plant and if I can go another month without it dying, I might get a second one but still. . ." Jessie rambled on while her father sat back in his chair and rolled his eyes. "Mom hated it here. I never wanted to end up like her. Feeling like I missed out on something."

"Jessie. Do you mean to tell me you've been traveling all these years because you thought that was what your mother wanted to do?"

"Well, in a way." That it came as a shock to him, surprised her.

"Why would you do that?" His eyebrows lifted. "She didn't hate it here."

"Don't you remember? It was all mom talked about." Jessie shook her head. "She dreamed of traveling. Seeing the world."

The waitress returned with their salads but Jessie no longer felt like eating.

"Did you know your mom was a stewardess when I met her?" Sparky rested an elbow on the table.

"What? Wait." That was news to her. "No. Never."

"Well, she was when we met." Her dad had a faraway, dreamy kind of look on his face.

"Go on." Jessie picked up her fork but still didn't want to take a bite fearful she might miss something.

"I was at a conference in Chicago. Your mother was staying at the same hotel with the rest of the crew. When I saw her across the room, I thought she was the most beautiful woman I'd ever seen. Still do. And that flight attendant uniform." He let out a whistle. "Almost stopped my heart. We talked for hours and it turned out she lived not too far from here."

"I knew that and she said that was why she wanted to see the world. She'd spent her youth in a small, hick town." Jessie used air quotes for the hick part. That's why they lived in Charleston, more conveniences and nearer to shopping. "Why didn't she continue flying?"

"Your brother happened." He winked.

"What?" Her eyes widened. This wasn't the story she grew up knowing.

"I skipped the conference and we spent the whole weekend together. We exchanged numbers and called each other every day after that. With her on the go, I didn't think we had much chance for a future. That was until she called in tears a few months later. She was pregnant with Travis."

"Gramps must have been furious." Her grand-parents were hugely religious and could not have taken that news with happiness.

"She was terrified of telling them. So much so, we agreed to get married right away. Met at the courthouse, signed the papers, and moved in that afternoon."

Jessie knew they didn't have a church wedding but it never dawned on her why. There was only one picture. Her dad in a suit and her mother in a simple white dress.

"It was tough going in the start. She had a career she loved and all those plans were swept away rais-ing a family." Sparky sighed.

"Marrying young and having a family, she never

got the chance after that." Her parents were both in their early twenties when they married. That she did know.

"Your mother had traveled plenty but it was hard when she'd get postcards from her friends who were still flying and seeing fancy places."

"We took that all away from her." It was guilt they all felt whether it was intended or not. A guilt that her father had never seemed to notice. Or maybe she had just interpreted things the way she wanted to see it all these years.

Sparky reached across and patted her hand with his. "No, you didn't. The day after we were married, I went to the bank and opened an account for her."

"A checking account?" Jessie questioned.

"No, a savings account. Not that it made a difference. I deposited several thousand dollars in there. Enough money at that time for her to go anywhere in the world and do anything she wanted to with it. Yes, we had a child on the way but it was there if she ever wanted to go. At any time."

Jessie rested her chin on her fist. This was all news to her.

"It's still there." He frowned.

"I don't understand. We were old enough. Mom could have gone anytime she wanted to." None of this made sense to her.

"Yes, she could've but she never did." He father looked off in the distance. "I often asked why and she would just shrug her shoulders and say she had too much to do here."

"That's crazy."

"Is it? Sometimes we complain about not getting to do things because we're too afraid to actually do them. As much as she talked about traveling, I couldn't get her to leave. Even booked a flight to Mexico one year as a surprise and she said no."

That she did remember, and they were all in shock that the trip didn't happen.

"I think she knew somehow, someway that her years were numbered and she didn't want to miss a minute of being with you kids. Jill lived life to the fullest. Some might call her a flirt but she appreciated and loved life, people, and most of all us. Maybe her sharing her dreams of travel was her way of encouraging you to follow your dreams whether they be here or somewhere else." Her dad was always a man of wisdom.

"Now I'm questioning what my dreams really are. I don't know where I belong anymore." She choked on the words. "I'm thirty-three years old and I feel like I've been wandering all this time in search of something and I still don't know what that is."

"I think you know, dear." This time he covered her hand with his. "You didn't need to come back for me. I'm glad you did but truth be told, I think you just wanted an excuse to come home and didn't want to admit it."

Silence followed as she pondered his words. Despite the awkwardness of her relationship with her boss, the past few weeks had been some of the most rewarding she'd had in a long time. Truth be true, she was damn sick of living out of suitcase.

"How are things at work?" Her dad's words startled her from her thoughts.

"Good. I like it." No, she loved it.

"You know BJ played against Ben in baseball."

Oh god, that's all she needed to hear. They'd finally talked about their ages last night. He was six years younger than her.

"I remember when his dad would bring him by. Nice kid."

"He's not a kid anymore."

"And neither are you. I think you two would be a good match."

"What?" Where did that come from? "You're trying to set me up with my boss."

"The guys at the gas station told me they saw you two kissing at a ball game a while ago."

Her face turned as red as her hair. "That's before I started working there. He has a no dating coworkers' policy." She rolled her eyes.

"Policies can be amended," he argued. "Since when did you ever play by the rules?"

"Like you said, he's Ben's age." Not that she minded but some people might.

"So what? Men die earlier than women, you'll have more years together." Jessie coughed on the iced tea she'd ordered. Leave it to her dad to see the practicality in everything.

"I'll keep that in mind. Whatever happened with the account you set up for mom? The travel one?"

"I divided it up three ways. Travis got his when he married and you and Ben will get yours when you do."

"Ben will probably get married before I do." The guy was a chick magnet.

"I don't know about that. I went to a conference never expecting to meet the love of my life and look what happened."

Her thoughts returned to BJ again as they seemed to more often that she wished. It was a lot to take in.

"Maybe you already met the love of your life and don't even know it yet," Sparky added.

"I don't know about that." It was still complicated.

"What I do know is that any man that ends up with you will be the luckiest man alive." Her dad always knew the right thing to say to make her feel better.

Tears watered her eyes. To think she could have lost this sweet man while out on the road. If that didn't make her want to stay before, she had two reasons now. Her dad and BJ. Her heart would stop beating if she'd lost one and it beat faster just thinking about the other.

CHAPTER FIFTEEN

~ *JESSIE* ~

THE STORE LOCK CLICKED. THE shop now stood dark and silent. Jessie walked to the front counter and sighed. The week had passed in a blur. Ever since her talk with dad, her mind had been in a tizzy. She could barely sleep and seemed to be walking in a haze. BJ had hardly been around and there was still so much to figure out.

Jessie grabbed what she needed from the cash area, hit the light switch and headed toward the hallway that led to her office. A light glowed from under BJ's office door, his deep voice conversing with someone on the phone. Was it Kayla?

Damn, she had to stop this insecurity and stop it now. When had she ever backed down from a challenge? Ever let anything or anyone stop her from achieving a goal? In that moment she realized what her dream was. Sometimes it took losing everything, to figure out what was most important. She had no idea if there was a future with BJ but there was no way she'd spend another minute wondering about it.

Her arms full of purchase orders and receipts, she

bumped her office door open with her hip, and tossed the armload on the desk. Her eyes searched the room. There. On the file cabinet. A bottle of champagne, a celebratory gift from her brothers. She took a quick look in the mirror, unbuttoned the top button of her blouse, and let down her hair. A determined face stared back. She smiled. Lightness filled her body, her spirit uplifted. She would get her man or die trying. Perhaps lose her job trying but she could get another job. There was only one BJ.

Jessie snatched the bottle, two plastic cups and proceeded to his office. Sauntered in, she rested her backside on his desk and kicked off her shoes. She waited for him to get off the phone before speaking. "Hey, boss. Working late?"

He leaned back in his office chair and looped his hands behind his head.

"Come on in, Jessie. Make yourself at home. Is it happy hour?" BJ cracked a smile.

Her heart skipped a beat. That killer smile got her every time. She inhaled the spicy scent of his cologne, momentarily at a loss for words.

"Maybe." Her lower lip extended just a tad. "My feet hurt and I thought this might take the edge off."

BJ loosened his tie and grabbed her nearest foot. His strong hands rubbed the aching ball of her foot, the massage pumping blood and heat to even the farthest reaches of her body. Bliss, the only word she could think of at the moment.

She reached for the champagne, looked intently

in his eyes and said, "We had a great day today. Month actually. All your projections have been met. Exceeded actually." She was rattling but that's what she did when something was really important to her. "We need to celebrate. You should be very happy with what you have accomplished."

"It's not what I have accomplished, but what we have accomplished." He emphasized the "we" and grabbed for her other foot.

"Well, in that case, I would like to renegotiate my contract."

His nimble fingers stopped.

She clutched the bottle to her chest. Words don't fail me now, she pleaded.

"About that." BJ frowned. "You're fired."

"I quit." She said at the same time. *Huh?*

"What?" BJ stilled. "I thought you liked it here. Isn't this what you always wanted to do?" A look of total disbelief spread over his face.

"Yes, it is, so why would you fire me? What the hell, BJ?" Jessie piped up.

Here she was hoping he'd beg her to stay and change the policy and he was firing her!

"You are the best, Jessie. Better than anyone I could hope for to help run this business. But I can't be here every day." He ran his fingers through his hair. "Watching you, wanting you, that part of our relationship ends now." He'd just echoed the same painful words he had said to her not so long ago. "Why are you quitting?"

She'd entered his office with seduction in mind but she wanted more. "As much as I love the job, I, too, want our relationship back. I want to see how far we can go. Not just for a weekend, but for however long it takes." She shrugged and let the foot he was holding slide down his inner thigh. "I don't want to stand along the side of the road waiting for something, or someone to show up when what I've been waiting for is already in front of me. If that means giving up my job, so be it."

"Then we agree we want to be together?" BJ asked. "Are you still quitting?"

"Am I still fired?" Jessie frowned.

"I technically wasn't going to fire you, more like promoting you."

"Huh?" Where was he going with this? This was the most mixed up conversation she'd ever had.

"I did a little rewording of the no dating policy. I'm firing you from assistant manager and rehiring you to manager. Your new contract doesn't have that clause in it."

"But that's your job. You're the manager."

"Not anymore and technically I'm the owner so I can do whatever I want."

"I don't understand where you're going with this?" Call her slow but it was too important to misinterpret anything.

"It's simple. I want you to stay. Not just until your dad is better but for good. Give us a chance and see where it goes. Give up your old job, take the new one. We can see each other every night and weekend. I want to go on dates. Ball games, movie nights in bed, fishing trips."

"It all sounds wonderful but we'll also be seeing

each other every day here. Will there be an issue with the staff?"

"No, I'm going back to the garage. You will take over everything here. I can't be in two places at one time."

It was what she wanted. Not that he would no longer be here, but that they would have a chance at being together.

"So, what do you think? Are you willing to stay and take the new job?" The hold he had on her foot increased as if he was willing her to take the offer.

"Yes. Yes!" He had no idea how much she wanted to stay.

BJ rose and framed her face in his hands. "Do you know how long I've waited to hear you say those words? The last month has been hell. Buddy misses you and I haven't had a decent night's sleep since you left." His face burned with desire. "I want you back in my life, in my bed."

"You do?" She jumped to her feet.

"I was on my way to your office to tell you the same thing." He leaned and kissed her forehead. "That was one of my mechanics on the phone. He can't handle things by himself so I'll be starting there again next week and you'll be running the show here." BJ hugged her tightly. "I don't want to spend another minute apart from you."

Her eyes lowered, lingering on his lips. His mouth inched closer. The soft kiss erased every ounce of tension that had filled her body the last few weeks. He tasted of peppermint gum, sweet and fresh as he nipped her lower lip. The kiss intensified. BJ's tongue teased and taunted while one hand slid between her thighs and the other cupped her breast. They were right back where they'd started and it felt right.

Jessie moaned as his thumb brushed a nipple and his lips nipped an earlobe.

"I've wanted you for so long." His voice vibrated along her throat, creating an avalanche of heat flowing to her core. She ached to have him inside, holding him tight.

"I don't want to wait either." Jessie grabbed for his waistband, unbuttoned the top button and unzipped the zipper. He grabbed her wrists and stood up.

"I'll be right back." He rushed from the room.

"Where are you going?" Jessie was breathless and instantly cold without his touch.

BJ trotted back into his office, condom packets in hand. "I had a condom machine installed in the men's bathroom," he stated before continuing the sensual assault of her lips.

Her swollen breasts pressed against his hard chest. Breathing hard, she came up for air and looked at his handsome face. "I don't want to wait any longer. Make love to me now." She pushed him toward the couch and collapsed on top of him.

"Yes, ma'am." He laughed, lifting his hips so she could slide his pants down easier. His engorged penis sprang loose.

Jessie trembled as she bent to taste the salty tip.

He groaned and reached for her. "Jessie, I need

you."

She rose, slid her skirt higher, and tossed her red thong to the side. Her eyes locked on his. She inched closer, hovering above him. Jessie's leg quivered as she felt the head of his hard length touch her wet core. How long she had yearned for him, dreamed of him. Slowly, she lowered, inhaling the scent of her arousal along the way. Buried to the hilt, she finally exhaled. Blood thundered in her head. Drunk with emotion, her head rolled back, a flush heating her chest.

She gyrated slowly at first, a sensual dance only meant for one man. Desire filled her every sense. She clutched the muscles of his arms, heard the deepening of his breath. Her body danced on its own, no longer under her control. Spinning out of control, the only thing holding her in place was BJ's grip on her thighs.

Vaguely aware that the cries of passion came from her lips, her gaze returned to his. Eyes filled with love and desire penetrated her heart and sent her flying over the edge. BJ's orgasm joined hers, filling her core with warmth. She collapsed in his arms. Tender kisses touched her forehead as strong arms held her close. "I hope this will be part of my new benefit package."

"Honey, you can have anything you want."

CHAPTER SIXTEEN

~ *JESSIE* ~

One year later

JESSIE FROWNED AS SHE FINISHED entering sales totals in the computer. The business had thrived so well they had to hire more people. She leaned back in the chair and plucked one of Buddy's hairs from her leopard print skirt. Things had been good, great, actually, with BJ. At least they had been until last week. Something had changed. Whatever it was, he wasn't sharing it with her.

Was he tired of her? Was there someone else? Did he need space? Ugh. Her gaze landed on a wall plaque that proclaimed, 'If it has tires or testicles it's gonna give you trouble'. How true was that? She could get new tires but there was no replacing BJ. Her heart sank. No matter what, they would talk tonight. Whatever the problem was, it could be fixed.

Her determination renewed, she locked her office and headed for home—their home. She'd moved in with him a few short weeks after they had had that important talk in his office. They got along wonderfully. Heck, even their families liked each other. What more could you ask for?

She always enjoyed the drive home. It brought back so many pleasant memories. The baseball stadium, the spot she had her flat tire, the shop where they had found shelter from a storm and engaged in newfound passion. It never failed to calm her after a stressful day, but today she was strung tighter than a bungee cord.

BJ sat, waiting for her on the front step, arms crossed and resting on his knees. Not a frown or smile on his face to forecast his mood and Buddy sat obediently by his side. She swallowed. Her hands shook when she grabbed her purse from the seat.

"What's wrong?" she asked, walking toward the house. Her legs trembled.

"Nothing's wrong." He patted Buddy.

"BJ, you're scaring me, something isn't right. Please tell me what's wrong? You've been quiet all week, and you were gone when I got up." She held her hands up and looked to the sky. "Whatever it is, we'll work it out." She sat down on the step, rested her head on his shoulder.

"I'm sorry. I didn't mean to scare you. It's me who's scared." Her put his arm around her and pulled her close.

"You? Why would you be scared?" Her heart stopped. "Has something happened? Is someone dying?"

"No, no. Nothing like that. I wanted to surprise you with something and I just hope you like it." Jessie exhaled the breath she'd been holding as he kissed her cheek and pulled her to standing.

"You didn't have to get me anything, and if you did, I'm sure I will love it." He often left her surprises and she loved every one of them.

BJ opened the door and guided her inside. "It's above the fireplace." He motioned and trailed behind her.

She walked slowly and quietly to the fireplace. Her eyes took in the details of the new painting that hung there. It was her, at least a little younger version of her. She was standing in front of her dad's garage, wearing her favorite outfit from those days; a tight yellow T- shirt, daisy dukes, and her turquoise and brown cowboy boots. "I don't understand. That's me. Where did you get this picture?"

BJ stood behind her. His arms wrapped around her waist.

"I saw the photo at your dad's place and I had a guy in Charleston paint it for me."

"Oh, how my brother hated that outfit. He was always yelling at me, 'Put some clothes on, Jessie.' It's amazing, but I still don't understand why you did it." She laughed and smiled up at the painting.

"I don't know if you remember but I was the kid that almost fell out of the truck watching you one day."

That moment in time flashed before her eyes. She remembered that day like it was yesterday and he'd been a part of it. It was the day she left and determined to never return. Today she couldn't imagine leaving unless it was with BJ by her side.

"I do remember. That was you?" Was it fate that had caused him to be there that day and set their lives in motion?

"Yeah. Broke my favorite pair of shades but it was worth it."

"Wait." Jessie paused. "Why did you go see my dad? Is he really okay?"

"Sparky's fine." BJ brushed it off. "Never better."

"Then why where you there?" Her fingers traced the deep brown frame. The painting was lovely and straight from the heart.

"I had to get permission." His voice cracked.

"Permission for what?" She turned and found him kneeling on the floor. Jessie clutched her hand to her chest. The room spun. Her heart pounded a hundred miles an hour.

"To ask for his daughter's hand in marriage." He held up a stunning ring. A bold chocolate brown pearl surrounded by diamonds. It was just her style, class with sass. Her mouth opened but no words escaped.

"Jessie Knutson, do you remember the first night you were here and I told you about my first love, the one that had the same color hair as you?" His words raised the hairs on the back of her neck. Her heart skipped a beat and tears ran down her cheeks.

"Yes."

"I didn't realize it at the time but that girl *was* you, Jessie. You were the girl I saw from my dad's pickup, the one I never stopped thinking about. It never dawned on me until you said you were Sparky Knutson's daughter. It was in the back of my mind all this time and when I went to see your father, I saw this picture and I knew we were meant to be together." She could see the moisture in his eyes and she sat down on his knee.

"Jessie Knutson, will you make me the happiest man in the world and be my wife?" His palm cupped her cheek.

"Yes!" She beamed and threw her arms around his neck. Happiness poured from her soul. She couldn't stop hugging and kissing her future husband. Even Buddy barked and joined in the party.

"I will never stop loving you. I think I always have," BJ confessed.

"I'll always love you too." Tears rolled down her face. "You know, I've driven for miles always looking for something and not knowing what. I now know what I was searching for and it was here all the time. *You* were here all the time."

BJ picked Jessie up in his arms, swung her around, and carried her across the room.

"Wait. You're going to make me dizzy," she squealed. "Where are you taking me?"

"Out to the garage to celebrate." BJ's smile shone as bright as her own.

"The garage?" She was laughing and crying at the same time.

"Yes. I just put in a new work bench. I thought we would break it in." BJ spun her around again. "You know, for old time's sake."

"BJ, put me down," she exclaimed as he set her on the kitchen counter. She held his face in her hands and gazed adoringly into his eyes. "I love

you, Bernard Spencer."
"I love you, too, Jessie, then, now, and forever."

AUTHOR'S NOTE

When I finished this short story, I had many readers wanting more. With the help of my friend and fellow writer Ryan O'Leary we came up with a Christmas story to go with it.

Getting Busy for
CHRISTMAS

By
Ginger Ring
And
Ryan O'Leary

To all the readers of
GETTING DOWN TO BUSINESS
who didn't want Jessie and BJ's story to end.

CHAPTER ONE

~ *BJ* ~

BJ SPENCER FROZE MID-SENTENCE AS he heard the stomp of his fiancée, Jessie Knutson's, high-heeled boots. Her boots stomped on the tile floor like a runway model's. A whiff of Sexy Little Things, her favorite lingerie store perfume, tickled his nose.

Damn, she had on his favorite outfit, too. A grey striped sweater dress which hugged every curve tighter than a race car driver at Talladega. She knew how to work it. That's for sure. Always did and always would. Those hips rocked side to side. Long red hair, wavy and unkempt, like she'd just rolled out of bed and she probably had.

Every head in the store turned as Jessie saun-tered by. A domino effect so to speak. A quart of oil slipped through a guy's hand, hit the floor, cracked opened, and oozed out in a puddle. Son of a . . . He hated to use the "you break it you bought it thing" but the innocent kid hadn't stood a chance.

Jessie represented class with sass. She could change a truck tire dressed in a pair of high heels and a skimpy pair of shorts, all the while sipping a glass of Kentucky whiskey and keeping up with game scores on the radio. His love for her knew no end.

"Ain't that your fiancée, BJ?" his customer asked.

"Yup." His fiancée and he were partners in a Charleston, West Virginia auto parts business, B & J's Auto Supply. They'd changed the name after getting engaged.

"Dang, she's a pistol, that one." The guy rolled his eyes and chuckled.

"Pistol? Hell, she's an AK-47 assault rifle with unlimited ammo." A smile crossed his lips. Not only was she a pistol, she loved guns. Having grown up with all brothers, Jessie could handle a firearm better than everyone he knew.

Nothing was better than going into the woods target shooting with her, her hair pulled back in a camouflage baseball hat, tight jeans, and knee boots. There wasn't a target she couldn't hit. The rush she got from shooting, and he from watching, always resulted in a heated balls to the wall — or tree, fuck fest on the way back.

He loved his little fire-cracker. Heat hit his belly as he remembered the time she waltzed into his office and sat cross legged on his desk. The little bit of her thigh that showed sported a new tattoo, the numbers and letters of one of her favorite guns 35mm. Hell. He almost fired off a load right in his pants. It was a fiery business meeting he'd never forget.

His eyes blurred as he double-checked the codes on the windshield wipers he held in a tight grip.

"These are the ones you need for your truck. Anything else I can get for you today?"

"Nope, looks like you got your hands full. Have a Merry Christmas, BJ and say hi to your dad for me." He exchanged the wipers for a handshake.

"Thanks. You too, Bob." BJ patted him on the back and greeted another customer. Fortunately, they didn't need any help. Bob was right. He did have his hands full. Jessie was rarely upset, but he could tell by the stomp that the woman was pissed with a capital P, and he knew the reason why.

Their second Christmas together had not gone as smooth as the first. Business was good but with the economy so tight, they were all putting in extra-long hours and working hard. He was back at the shop for now. Taking the morning shift before going to the garage. Jessie came in for the late afternoon to closing time stint. Buddy, their dog, probably spent more time sleeping in bed with her than he did.

Straightening his aching back, BJ headed for her office. He gave the closed door a quick one knuckle knock before opening it. Jessie faced away, slightly bent over some papers on the desk. He recalled their first encounter on the work bench of his garage. He appreciated the view of her heart-shaped ass and leaned against the doorframe. She'd changed a little in the past year. Put on a few pounds in all the right places. Now that she was eating home cooked meals and not living on fast food salads and gas station coffee, she'd bloomed into a bombshell.

He still stared at her ass as she pivoted, lifted her hem a few inches, and sat on the desk. What, no panties? The temperature of the small room shot up a hundred degrees.

"Enjoying the view from back there, boss?" Her sultry low voice thrilled him every time. His dick grew an inch with every word. He was fucked.

After checking the hall behind him, BJ shut the door and flipped the lock. "I'm enjoying the view from up front just as much, boss." Equal partners in everything, they still relished the battle about who was really in charge. His hands itched to touch her smooth skin. An index finger skimmed along the back of her thigh while the thumb of his other hand caressed her lip. "I've missed you so much."

"You just saw me this morning." Jessie flirted and arched her back. The tips of her boobs brushed his chest. He groaned and ran his fingers through her thick, silky hair.

"Yeah but I didn't get to do this." The second his lips touched hers he was lost. Kissing her was heaven on earth. His tongue slipped in, she tasted sweet, like sugar and cinnamon, all rolled into one. Jessie moaned or was that him? Her hands grabbed his ass and pulled him closer. He nipped her lips and kissed her once more before forging a trail to her ear. Jessie's soft breaths on his neck sent a shiver down his spine.

She wiggled on the desk. Her scent of arousal overtook the room, overtook him. His lips blazed a trail to her neck and the pulse of her heart beat at a frantic pace. He grazed her breast. Jessie squealed. Good thing the shop was busy or someone might have come running. "You have the best tits." BJ cupped them in both hands to squeeze and massage. No wonder they called boobs "sweater puppies", he could pet them all day long.

"We really shouldn't be doing this, but I couldn't wait any longer." Jessie managed to get out between moans. She struggled to unbutton his shirt.

"I know what you mean." He rubbed her nipple to a peak through the sweater, and she whimpered. "All these long hours. Not to mention all those extra toys and things to sell."

Jessie stilled. "What do you mean all those extra toys to sell?"

"You know. The toy cars, tool sets, the T-shirts." Why were they talking? His only concern was how soon he could be inside this glorious woman.

"I thought you wanted those things in the store?" She framed his face with her hands and looked him square in the eye.

Uh oh, not good. Now for damage control.

"I do. It's a great idea but it's also an extra expense and something we have a short time span to sell." BJ kissed her nose. "Can we talk about this some other time? These are the only toys I'm interested in right now."

Jessie scoffed.

He held a breast in each hand. "Oh, shit. You're not wearing a bra either." An animal groan escaped from his throat.

Green eyes that had flashed with passion, now sparked with anger. Two tight fists settled on each side of her lovely hips.

"Jessie. What's wrong?" Her lower lip bent in a sexy pout and he crushed her in a big bear hug.

"I'm tired and sexually frustrated."

"I can help you with the second one." Goose-bumps rose on her silky skin as his fingers caressed along her thighs to her pussy. Her hips bucked.

A loud knock shook the door. "Hey, boss. You in here?" The spell broken, their foreheads touched, their passion put on hold.

"Yes." They answered, gazing into each other's eyes and smiling.

"We could use some help out here." An urgent tone was conveyed in his voice.

"Be right there," BJ answered. He kissed her forehead. "To be continued," he promised before pulling her skirt back down.

"I hope so." Jessie glanced at the floor. Her legs crossed and she rested her chin on the palm of her hand.

"As soon as the holidays are over let's go away for the weekend. Book a hotel and not leave the room." He gave her a quick kiss on the cheek.

"Hmmm. Sounds like heaven. I can't wait." Jessie rose to her feet and smoothed her hair back.

"Are we good, Jessie?" He held a nervous breath.

"Yes, like I said I'm just worn-out and tired of not seeing much of each other. Thankfully, Christmas only comes once a year." A shy smirk crossed her kiss swollen lips. She set her hands at her waist and her hard nipples showed through the sweater.

"I hope you have a bra with you, or maybe not

with attributes like those." He glanced at her chest. "Those guys will buy anything." He winked.

She scowled. Damn. He'd meant to tease but this was not the day to bait.

"My attributes are up here." Her well-manicured finger tapped her forehead.

"In my eyes, you have attributes everywhere." He flashed a killer smile that never failed to bring her over to his side. It didn't work.

Her eyes narrowed. "You think men buy from me because they like the way I look?" An invisible glove had just been thrown on the office floor.

"Red, I'd buy anything you have to sell, but if a guy really wanted to know something mechanical, they know who to talk to." His non-manicured finger indicated that that guy was him. The killer smile switched to devilish smirk. She'd lured him and he'd gladly taken the hook.

"Is that so?" Those smoking hot legs sauntered ever so slowly to the other side of the desk. An elegant finger traced along the edge. The leather office chair creaked as she sat. "So, what do you say? Are you up to a little friendly wager as to who can rack up more sales?"

She crossed her legs, the scene reminiscent of a certain Basic Instinct movie. He swallowed. Ms. Stone was fierce but she couldn't hold a candle to Ms. Jessie Knutson. The wager excited him as much as it appeared to excite her. He'd played right into her hands and loved every minute of it. BJ placed both hands on the desk and leaned in.

"I'll take that bet. So, what do I get when I win?"

Confidence was something he'd never lacked.

Jessie dismissed his response. "When I win you have to do anything that I want you to." She interlocked her slender fingers.

"Would this be of a sexual nature?" He hoped.

"Of course." Her eyes narrowed and her cheeks flushed a pretty pink.

A win-win situation if he ever saw one. "Agreed." He reached a hand across the desk to seal the deal. "And when I win, you have to do anything I want you to do."

"And would this be of a sexual nature, also?" White teeth showed as she bit her lip.

"Of course." The deal was made.

Jessie stood and shook his hand in a firm grip. "Game on, big boy. You're going down."

"I certainly hope so." BJ winked and walked to her side. "Now get that pretty little ass out there." He spanked her playfully on the behind. "Oh, and put a bra on. Those gorgeous tits are mine," he declared before leaving.

The challenge had her as wound up as he was. He knew her body language well. When she swung her foot back and forth it was the equivalent of a cat twitching their tail. All worked up and ready to pounce. This was one competition he would enjoy, win or lose.

CHAPTER TWO

~ *JESSIE* ~

CLAD IN ONLY A PAIR of boots, Jessie tossed the sweater dress to the side. BJ Spencer. Saying his name drove a sizzle from head to toe. She loved that man with all her heart. Little did she know when her car had a flat a year and a half ago, her soulmate would show up in a tow truck.

Lately, however, working different shifts had put a cramp in their love life. They'd not had sex in over a week. A lifetime in their young relationship. Her plan to seduce him in her office had been interrupted. A smile lit across her lips. The contest was a spur of the moment thing but a great idea. Now they had something to look forward to. The fact that it would help sales didn't hurt either.

Digging in a file cabinet, she found a beige bra and panty set. It was always best to be prepared in case something got torn during an after-hours love session. She pulled a pink T-shirt over her head, zipped up a tan skirt, and put her hair in a French twist. Not her usual style but this meant business. She was determined to use her mental attributes to win, and not her physical ones.

The place was packed when she walked up front. Her first stop was the cashiers' desk. She checked to make sure they had everything they needed. Change, register tape, did anyone need water or a bathroom break? Her employees came first because a happy employee equaled a loyal and dedicated employee. Her next stop was the sales floor.

"Hey, Jessie. How ya doing?" An older gentleman captured her attention.

It was Walt, one of her dad's longtime friends and a confirmed bachelor. She'd always enjoyed their talks whenever her route landed her at his body shop's garage door.

"Walt. It's great to see you. How have you been?" Jessie greeted him with a big hug and kiss on the cheek.

"Great, except the truck is taking a shitter on me. Need some new spark plugs and ran out at the shop." He scratched his nose. "That new guy isn't on top of things like you were."

"Thanks, it takes a while to get a handle on what everyone needs and when. So you got a lady friend yet?" A comment she always teased him with whenever they stopped to gossip about friends and family. But this time the question turned his cheeks as red as his stocking hat. "Hmm. Walt, you got a little quiet there. Come on. Who is she?" Her hands settled on her hips and she tapped her foot on the floor.

"Well, you remember Connie from church? Doug's widow." His face now turned bright scarlet as he pretended to study the spark plugs even though he held the right ones in his hand. "It's been a couple years since he passed." He waved the package as he talked. "And, well, we were talking one day and I asked her out to dinner."

"Good for you. How long have you been going out?" She knew Connie had been lonely for a long time after her husband died in a car accident, so she couldn't be happier for them.

"Oh, since September." Walt smiled. His love showed.

"Did you get her a Christmas present yet?" Jessie beamed.

"I'm not good at that stuff. My niece, she works at a jewelry store, helped me pick out a nice necklace for her, but I thought I'd get her a couple other things too. Women like gifts. Don't they?" He itched his nose again. A nervous habit she hadn't noticed before. Or maybe he was just uncomfortable with the subject. She wasn't sure but it was cute.

"They love gifts." New love, no matter what the age, made her giddy. His good mood spread to her big-time.

"Hey, I like your shirt, Jess. Where'd you get it?" Walt indicated her outfit.

She wore one of the T-shirts BJ had just complained about. A cute short sleeve pink T-shirt that read, "Classy Chassy" across the front. It had bling. The words were in glitter with sparkles and rhinestones here and there.

"Well, you're in luck, Walt. We sell them here. We also have a few nightshirts." She leaned in and whispered in his ear. "You know, in case her truck takes a shitter and she needs to stay overnight." By the time they left the aisle Walt's face was aflame. He bought one in every color plus some toy trucks for Connie's grandsons.

BJ stood, with arms crossed, and watched as she helped carry some of Walt's packages out to his vehicle. 'People loved to buy. They don't want to be sold.' A quote she remembered from a former sales class. It filled her with contentment to assist people in finding what they needed and having them be pleased with what they bought. She walked on air as she passed through the door again. BJ still studied her, a slight scowl on his face and one hand on his hip.

She couldn't help herself. She strutted up and poked him in the chest. Just like she had before the first time they'd kissed. "And that, Mr. Spencer, is how it's done."

"Yes, ma'am." He grabbed her hand and held it to his chest. It was another déjà vu moment from their first encounter and the first time she told him how much she hated to be called ma'am.

Jessie was energized by the rivalry and enjoying every minute of her victory. Her eyes locked on his. If only the room hadn't been filled with a ton of people, she'd drag him to her office and take full advantage. Her hand slipped from his warm grasp. "I'd love to stand and chat, but I've got a contest to win." She winked and strolled away. Her mind clicked with possible ideas for triumph. She bit her lip and surveyed the store. There. Of course. Over along the wall. Her leather pumps rushed to the apparel section.

Jessie gathered an armload of pink shirts and distributed them amongst the female employees. "Here girls, an early Christmas present from the shop." Some excited cries were mingled in the midst of "thank you", and "awesome". "If you love them, your customers will love them, too. Let's wear these shirts every day while talking them up, and the toys too."

"Can I put mine on right now?" The newest helper, a brunette college student, spoke up. "You have no idea how badly I wanted one of these."

"Of course. Let's rock these shirts and show the boys how it's done. Great job, everyone." Jessie watched her crew head to the back room to change and searched for any customers needing help.

Pleased as pie with her new strategy, she spied BJ marching her way. Still as handsome as the first time she'd laid eyes on him. Tall, lean, and, in her eyes, drop dead gorgeous. His dark brown hair was almost black except in the summer. His brown eyes smoldered. Oh, how she yearned to rub that five o'clock shadow along her skin. Nuzzle his face between her breasts and run her fingers through his thick, soft hair. Heat rushed to her face just thinking about it. She grabbed a nearby brochure on air filters and fanned herself.

"Do you feel all right, Jessie?" BJ pressed the back of his hand to her forehead. "You look a little red in the face."

"Nothing's wrong with me. I'm just charged up

thinking about all the wicked things I'm going to make you do when you lose." She caressed his cheek as she passed. Her core clenched. Oh, that stubble got her every time.

"About that." His hand clamped on her elbow. "What's with all the girls getting those T-shirts? You can't buy your way to winning."

"I'm not buying anything. The shop gave the shirts to them for Christmas." She tilted her jaw to the side.

"What? As owner of the place, I don't remember authorizing this." He scratched his chin with a business card he had in hand. The raspy scrape threatened to send her into a meltdown.

"Well, as *partner* of this operation, I decided it would be good for sales. A guy practically bought this one right off my chest." She aligned said shirt and puffed out her chest.

"I'd pay you to take your shirt off also, but it doesn't mean we should be giving them away." BJ appeared nervous.

"Don't worry. Look." A couple guys were being led to the display to look at styles and colors.

"Say, miss?" A guy tapped her on the shoulder. "Do you have more shirts like you got on? I'd like to get one for my wife."

"We sure do. Follow me." Jessie winked at her fiancé before leading the man away. "So, what size does she need?"

"Ah, I don't know. She's about your size only a little bigger." How many times had she heard that one?

"I'm sure we have just the one." She couldn't help the huge grin forming on her face. BJ was toast.

The next few hours flew by. Yes, the holidays were hectic but they were also a lot of fun. The time went quickly and she enjoyed selling. A swift glimpse at her watch told her it was nearing time for BJ to go home. Her heart sank. She hated to see him leave, but someone had to go home and let Buddy out.

Where was he anyway? She spied him at the checkout counter talking to the clerks. Her tired feet carried her to see what their meeting was about. She loved when he turned all business and rallied the troops. His hand rested on the counter while he spoke.

"Any more questions?" He quizzed the group.

The main cashier spoke up. "So, free washer fluid with a ten dollar purchase, and a free ice scrapper with a twenty five dollar purchase. Right, boss?"

"Yes, and make sure it's the big scrapper with the brush on the handle." Her man pointed to the display now set behind the counter.

"What's this? I don't think I heard of this promotion yet." She reached BJ's side and dragged him away to speak in private.

"Don't worry. I decided it would be good for sales." He gifted her with a quick kiss on the cheek and a suggestive smirk only she could witness. "All's fair in love and sales," he added in a deep voice only low enough for her to hear. He may be good, but she was still going to win.

~ *BJ* ~

WAS THERE A WORSE SOUND than an alarm clock going off when it is still dark outside? Fuck, no. BJ groaned and hit the switch before it could wake Jessie. Fortunately, there were only a couple more days of getting up at this god-forsaken hour. What idiot had the bright idea to open the shop at seven every day for the week of Christmas? He closed his eyes tighter. That idiot was him.

Jessie stirred and he snuggled in closer. His dick was hard as a baseball bat and ready to play extra innings. BJ's very happy forearm nestled between her warm, soft breasts. She slept naked, except for the socks. Jessie's feet were like ice. The socks were a must on their wood floors and in bed. So far, things were going great with the shop, and he'd bought Jessie a present he hoped she'd enjoy.

Still, she'd be angry as hell. They agreed to not buy gifts and just go away for a little trip instead. This gift was a necessity. A shudder shook him as he remembered that stormy night a few weeks ago when an early ice storm had hacked ten years off his life. Jessie should have been home by seven o'clock. When the clock struck seven-thirty, worry set in, and by eight o'clock, he was frantic. Her cell phone went straight to voicemail. When she hadn't arrived on time, the excuses in his head began. She must have gone shopping, stopped for gas, ran into a friend, or decided to pick up some takeout. Where was she?

He'd just darted out the door, truck keys in hand, to search for her when her headlights flashed down the driveway. A chill went down his spine just thinking about it. He'd made a few calls around town the next day. The result was a gift that would keep her safe and give him peace of mind.

Jessie snored softly. He chuckled. She only snored when exhausted or she'd had a little too much to drink. It didn't bother him though. Nothing was better than waking up next to the love of his life. He kissed her bare shoulder. The smell of vanilla tickled his nose, the shower gel she loved. She purred and cuddled closer. This would be tougher than he thought. He ached to be inside her. Sighing, he kissed her shoulder again and rolled out of bed. "Well, sleeping beauty, I got to go." BJ tucked the blanket close to her frame and positioned another fleece throw on top of her.

CHAPTER THREE

~ JESSIE ~

CHRISTMAS EVE DAY AT LONG last. Jessie yawned in the cool passenger seat and observed the white flakes dancing in the headlights. Fortunately, they were only supposed to get a dusting. All they needed was a whiteout on the last day of the Christmas shopping season and the final day of their bet. She burrowed into her warm coat and enjoyed the sideview of her charming driver. His hair was a little shorter than when they'd first met. He thought it made him look more professional. It made him look younger. Oh well, he was younger than her but it never made a bit of difference to them. BJ focused on her, his bright smile filling the cab of his truck. "Are you warm enough?"

"Yes."

"You're quiet this morning. Worried you're going to lose the bet?" His hand snuck over and squeezed her knee. Warmth spread like wildfire along the length of her limbs.

"No worries. I've got this one in the bag." Jessie grinned and reached across to do the same. Faith was something she seldom lacked.

"Think so, huh?" he volleyed.

"Know so," she returned.

The horizon blushed with the first hint of sunrise as they drove the twisting West Virginia roads to reach the main highway. The traffic was light this early in the day except for the few diehard shoppers and early morning risers out and about. They reached the store in record time and quickly opened the shop. It would be a short day. Today they worked the same shift, seven to four. BJ was wide awake but not Jessie. A mug of hot coffee was never far from her grasp.

The Christmas spirit and good mood of the season was contagious. The hectic pace and long hours of the shopping season would soon be at an end and things could finally get back to normal. Their crew had joined in the excitement of their contest, even if they didn't know what the fun was all about. A battle of the sexes was at hand. Since they had an equal ratio of male employees to female employees, the guys added their sales to BJ's total and the girls did the same with Jessie's. So far it was running neck and neck. The losing manager promised to foot the bill for a pizza party after the holidays.

The hours ticked away. The totals went back and forth. Jessie, high on caffeine and adrenaline, was on a roll. No one left the store empty handed. This was her element. Their customer traffic slowed after lunch. Jessie aligned a display of tools destroyed by a naughty four year old and noticed BJ observing her. He winked and wandered to the back room.

What was he up to?

Curiosity getting the best of her, she followed. Where had he gone? As she passed his closed office door, his low southern drawl could be heard coming through the door. Not wanting to interrupt, she stopped and waited. And waited. Ten minutes later, the door swung open. He snatched her hand and dragged her into his office. The door slammed shut and he pressed her against the wall.

"Spying on me?" There was mischief in his eye.

"No. I was just curious where you had gone." She tried to act nonchalant but his closeness never failed to make her tingle all the way to her toes. "I didn't think you would give up so easily," she goaded.

"I'm not giving up. I'm just in a hurry to have you naked and begging for more." His strong hand lingered on her jaw before it slid to her throat.

Her eyes closed. How could you miss someone so much when they were standing right in front of you? The rhythm of her heart thumped so loud she could feel it in her ears. The musky scent of his aftershave fired heat in her core. Her lips were dry. Eyelids half-closed.

"Hold that thought, my little cougar cat." He kissed her nose.

Jessie swallowed. "What thought?" She was not good at playing innocent but sometimes a girl just had to try.

"The 'I hope he takes me up against the wall' thought," he teased.

"I wasn't thinking that." She bit her lip.

His eyebrow lifted.

"I was thinking along the lines of 'over the back of the couch'." She smirked and lifted an eyebrow.

A full-on belly laugh shook him from head to foot. He backtracked to sit on the desk. "As much as I would love to do so, and believe me, I thoroughly plan to do that in the very near future. I just got off the phone with one of the local shelters. I called around to see if any places could still use a few toys or Christmas gifts, and I found one." He ran his fingers through his thick head of hair. "They're sending a truck over and it should be here soon, if they aren't already, to pick things up."

Jessie choked up and a sense of pride filled her. BJ had such a kind heart. They'd already said they would donate to different charities for Christmas instead of exchanging gifts, but she was excited about giving more. "What a fabulous idea."

"Hey, boss?" One of their employees knocked and yelled through the door.

"What?" they both echoed before laughing at their private joke.

"There's some guy here about picking up some toys."

"We'll be right there," BJ answered for the both of them.

Jessie hugged her man. Could she get any happier? They both left to help box up the toys. Jessie and the girls added some of the T-shirts, sweatshirts, and nightshirts to go for gifts also. Despite being tired, everyone had renewed energy.

The hours passed. Business wound down and

they dismissed their employees early. "Have a Merry Christmas, everyone." BJ walked their crew to the door where Jessie stood handing out envelopes containing a generous bonus to each.

"So, who won?" One of the girls stopped and asked.

BJ put an arm around Jessie's shoulder, "We all won. Pizza party in January for everyone." He tried again to usher everyone out. "Now, go home and have a Merry Christmas."

Jessie grinned from ear to ear and repeated his sentiments. They really were blessed. A growing business, loyal employees, a nice house, and each other. What more could she ask for?

To think it was not too long ago, she'd sat eating takeout in a lonely hotel room wishing for a place of her own and someone to share it with.

~ *BJ* ~

Finally, they were home. A roaring fireplace snapped in the other room and Jessie popped the cork on a bottle of champagne. BJ eyed the small package that leaned against the dresser mirror. Jessie had won the contest. Her request? He had to wear what was in the box.

He took a deep breath. This wasn't good. A box of playing cards was bigger. What had he got himself into? He shook his head and tore the Santa wrapping paper off. A red and green ribbon floated to the floor and he tossed the wadded-up paper to the trash can across the room. It bounced off the back rim and in. Score.

Cautiously, he opened the cover of the tiny square box and removed what was inside. WTF? Holding it up by one finger, he shook his head and frowned in the mirror. He was so fucked.

~ *JESSIE* ~

A piece of fresh birch popped in the fireplace as she took another sip of bubbly. The sight of red and yellow flames blending together and curling around the white bark of the wood was spellbinding. She was exhausted but being with BJ always renewed her energy. Jessie snickered. Had he opened the box yet? Buddy nudged her hand for a pet and she scratched his ears. A new bone and duck toy lay by his bed. "Where's your daddy, Buddy?" Buddy sneezed and plodded back to his bed.

The bedroom door opened. BJ's bare feet padded across the tile floor. An unreadable expression adorned his face. Arms crossed and a flannel blanket wrapped around his waist, he slumped in a dining room chair. How could someone look adorable and drop-dead sexy at the same time? A few strands of damp finger-combed hair stuck up here and there. The fresh, moist fragrance of shower gel drew her to her feet. Good, he hadn't shaved. Her cheeks flamed. The ticklish spot on her inner hip twitched in anticipation of the delicious scrape of his whiskers.

The long hours outside without a shirt could still be seen, his skin tan and tight. Everything a girl could possibly want under her tree or in her bed. Her pulse throbbed. Her core ached. A soft moan escaped as she traced the dark chest hair with her eyes. Jessie's slender fingers itched to follow the trail of dark curls as they disappeared beneath the blanket.

BJ cleared his throat. Her fantasies were put on hold.

"So, what did you think of my gift?" Jessie twirled a long ringlet of red hair around a graceful finger.

He stood. The blanket fell to the floor. Bronze skin glowed in the firelight. Wide shoulders she yearned to be held by. Strong, muscular arms and those graceful hands that could tear down an engine one minute and remove a sliver from Buddy's paw the next. Long, powerful legs graced with a dusting of soft hair. He was magnificence from head to toe and gloriously naked. Well, except for a bright red reindeer thong. The reindeer's nose was accented with a bell on the end. Brown antlers pointed out to the sides.

Jessie burst into laughter. Her hands covered her mouth. Tears threatened to fall. A brief moment in time she would never forget.

"It's not quite what I had in mind." He rested on one hip. The bell jingled prompting Buddy to raise his head. "Buddy. Out," he ordered. Buddy rose and stretched before tiptoeing his way down the hall to their bedroom. BJ's attention back on Jessie, he licked his lips and asked, "So what are you wearing under there? I hope it is equally as festive."

The flannel shirt dropped from her shoulders. Her only attire was a pair of wool socks. She blushed as he gave her the once-over. The intensity in his eyes made her core weep. A bell chimed loudly as the reindeer grew.

"My, Rudolph. What a big nose you have." Jessie giggled and BJ glanced at her jiggling breasts.

"Little Red." He approached. "I think you have your fairy tales and Christmas stories mixed up." His eyes lingered on places she yearned for him to touch.

He stood close. Springy chest hair caressed the tips of her hard nipples. A flush crossed her chest. Mariah Carey's sweet voice on the radio sang about what she wanted for Christmas. Cinnamon candles filled the room with their delicious, spicy fragrance.

Work-roughened fingers outlined her face. Her eyes half-closed with the intensity of his gaze. A soft kiss touched each lid, her forehead, and the tip of her nose. She swallowed. Those lips tasted her mouth. So sweet. So tender. How could one so strong be so gentle? Her heart soared. Her legs weakened. He pressed her against the counter. Rugged whiskers along her neck sent her heart racing.

She was falling, spinning out of control. Her legs

lifted out from under her, BJ carried her to the plush sheepskin lying by the fire. The shearing rug was soft and luxurious against her skin. A comfy pillow placed beneath her head.

"Have I told you how beautiful you are to me?" Her face blushed under his loving stare and devoted words. "It hurts to think that I might have spent my life without you and how lucky I am to have found you."

Her eyes misted. "We are both lucky."

"I can't hold out any longer. As much as I want to lose myself in your beautiful eyes, the rest of you is calling my name." He kissed her neck. Jessie leaned her head back, her hair grazing the smooth wood floor. When his lips found the side of her neck again and moved slowly around behind her ear, she sighed deeply.

"God, you smell so good," BJ whispered in her ear. "I could just eat you up."

"So, take a bite," Jessie said with a snicker.

BJ's lips curled back over his gleaming white teeth and he nipped her earlobe.

A shock rushed from her ear straight to her core. The ache throbbed deep. She bucked her hips and thrust her chest up, wiggling her bottom in the process.

BJ placed a firm hand on her stomach. "Where do you think you're going?"

Jessie opened her mouth to answer, but BJ's tongue began a slow descent down her collarbone and across the swell of her cleavage, suppressing the words she was about to speak.

"I need to feel you," Jessie exclaimed through gritted teeth as BJ's raspy cheek passed over her swollen left nipple.

She reached between his legs and found the head of his pulsing penis. Warm and smooth to the touch. The slit wet.

"Not so fast," BJ scolded and quieted her hand from further exploration.

She kicked her foot like a petulant child. "But I want it."

BJ placed her hand back on the floor and ran the tip of his finger down her side. Jessie's entire body quaked. She could feel the smear of pre-cum on the tip of her forefinger and she made another grab him.

BJ stopped her again. "I said not yet," he growled.

"But, B–"

"But nothing." There was unmistakable authority in his voice. He lifted her hand and moved to cover her with his big frame.

He took Jessie by the forearms and leaned her back slowly onto the soft fur of the rug. Jessie settled in nicely, and before she knew it, BJ had both her hands pinned to the floor above her head. Her entire body shook with erotic delight. She could feel him hover above her, holding himself up with one thickly muscled arm. She wanted to open her eyes and behold the way the fire illuminated his handsome face but was afraid she'd expire if she did.

BJ kissed another trail down between her breasts and went right. He flicked the tip of her perky nipple and Jessie cried out with ecstasy.

He licked it once more and moved back up to her neck. "My God, Jessie." He inhaled deeply. "Those perfect breasts of yours get me so *fucking* hard," he whispered in her ear.

Every nerve in Jessie's body danced with joy, every sense vibrated. She could smell the musky birch as it crackled in the blue flames beside her, hear the wind whipping through the nearly leafless willow trees just outside their door. She gave a powerful tug, attempting to free her hand from BJ's firm grip.

"You'll have to try harder than that, Red," he said with a chuckle.

Jessie opened her eyes and gazed up at him with immeasurable intensity. Damn! He looked even better in the firelight.

BJ's free hand moved to the heated spot between her legs. "Are you?" He pushed the tip of his middle finger into her and withdrew it with a smile. "Mmmm. You sure are. And you're hotter than that fire beside us."

"Why won't you let me have you?" Jessie whimpered.

"Because I want more of you first."

He pushed the tip of his finger back into her channel, but this time he pushed the rest of the digit as deep as he could go. Jessie stomped her foot on the ground and bit her lip. When BJ's warm mouth engulfed her left nipple and sucked, her body began to thrash.

BJ took his time with her, sliding his finger in

and out slowly while he lavished her nipples with attention. He licked one and then the other. He'd released her hands from his grip, but she barely noticed, too lost in pleasure to even care. He massaged one breast with his hand while tonguing the opposing nipple aggressively.

Jessie writhed on the floor underneath him, tangling her hair in the hands that were now free. She peeked and saw BJ's sable eyes blazing back up at her, his smooth, slick tongue dancing over her puffy nipples.

She reached for his head and snatched a handful of thick dark hair. "You have to stop, BJ."

He kissed the side of her breast. "Why?" He wiggled his finger inside her.

"Because," she began, but halted when he slipped a second finger into her pussy. "I'm going to explode if you don't."

BJ gave her a wicked grin and slipped his hands behind her thighs. "Well, I doubt this is going to help then."

He moved slowly down her body, tracing the lines of her stomach with his tongue.

"BJ. No." Jessie tugged on the hair in her hand. "You're killing me. I'll die."

He seemed to enjoy the pull of her fingers in his hair. "Nice knowing," he kissed the spot directly above her clit, "you."

Her posterior levitated off the soft rug and he buried his tongue deep inside of her.

"My God," BJ snarled. "You taste like honey fresh from the hive. I could dine on you for hours."

His words shot through Jessie's writhing body like a bullet train, spreading in her heart like a wildfire. Few things got her as heated as knowing that her man enjoyed her.

"Stop," Jessie huffed. "I'm going to…Oh My…God! Please, stop." She fought back the orgasm hammering at the door to be let out.

"Do it for me, Jessie," BJ said. His words garbled by the fluttering of his tongue and her hips swiveled and bucked.

Jessie couldn't fight it any longer, the orgasm flashed all over her body. She gripped the rug with strong hands and let the pent-up desire she'd felt for her sexy man overtake her.

BJ quickly sprang up from his spot down at Jessie's tender opening as she started to climax. Bright colors started to burst behind her eyes.

"Where are you going?" she asked between gasps of air.

BJ looked her deep in the eyes but didn't say a word. He pushed the tip of his thick cock into her slick opening and fell forward onto her chest. "I couldn't wait another minute," he whispered in her ear. Their connection was more than physical. The full sensation inside matched only by the completeness felt in her heart.

Jessie's arms closed around him and she pulled him close. Beside them the fire roared, the heat radiating off of it warming her sensitive skin. She held onto him tightly as he dipped his penis in and out with long, rhythmic strokes.

BJ pulled back. A boyish smile was on his face

and there was a lock of hair on his forehead. Jessie's legs unlocked from around his waist and lifted. He plunged into her to the hilt. Her cry of pleasure floated in the air. A slow withdrawal and then another push in. Each thrust built in intensity and speed. Sweat dripped from his forehead.

Her toes tingled. Her thigh muscles throbbed. Her breath came in gasps. She dug her nails into his back leaving marks that would surely be seen for days. Blood pounded in her ears.

"I can't take this anymore," BJ exclaimed. "You feel too good for me to hold-off any longer.

She pulled him back down to her by the hair. "Then do it for me. Now!"

Higher and higher she rose, another wave of pleasure about to come crashing down on her. The gasps and groans of her man had her teetering on the edge. A moment suspended in time before the world burst in a million colors. Wave after wave of pleasure rolled. The first surge of his cum spraying inside her, set Jessie off and she came again. BJ's thrusting slowed and he collapsed on top of her. Gathered her in his arms, his lips touched her skin and he nuzzled her neck.

"I love you, Jessie." Her heart sang.

"I love you, too." His arms held her tight.

CHAPTER FOUR

~ *JESSIE* ~

"GOOD MORNING, SLEEPYHEAD." BJ SWEPT the hair from her forehead and planted a kiss. He hugged her tightly and wrapped his leg around hers. They'd finally made it to bed and slept in late.

"Good morning." Jessie nestled in his arms. Was there a better feeling than spooning? Flesh to flesh. Her fingers fluttered along his leg. His arm hair sprang back as she caressed his warm skin. A hint of hazelnut coffee floated in the air. It's a wonder she remembered to set the coffee maker before going to bed. A vision of BJ in his Christmas attire caused the ends of her mouth to lift.

"What's that smile about?" His whiskers delighted the back of her neck with every word.

"I was just thinking about your reindeer outfit. You were such a good sport, better luck next time." She rolled onto her back and tweaked his nose.

"I hate to break it to you darling, but you really didn't win."

Her mouth dropped. "What?"

"I forgot to add in a late sale. Someone ordered

some mud flaps and floor mats for an SUV." A slow grin grew.

"I don't get it. How did that happen?" Jessie rose on an elbow and studied him.

"Because I was the customer."

She tilted her head. "That's cheating. Who's it for? We don't own an SUV."

"*We* don't but *you* do." BJ exited the bed and grabbed a robe. "It's in the shed." He left the room.

Jessie scrambled for some boots and wrapped herself in a thick blanket. "What? What are you talking about?" He kept going. "Hey, wait for me." She dashed to keep up.

BJ pulled on a pair of boots and plopped a fuzzy bomber hat on Jessie's head. It blocked her view and she shoved it into place. The door opened, Buddy bounded out the door bumping her and she almost lost her footing. "This is crazy. Slow down."

"Come on, slow poke." His boots crunched on the new snow. It sparkled like diamonds.

Jessie followed the large footprints as best she could. Buddy barked and ran in circles around them. A pair of cardinals caroled in a tree above. BJ tired of her slow pace and carried her fireman style the rest of the way. He hit the opener and the door rolled up. There sat her old sedan. The one whose flat tire had stranded her on the side of the road until her favorite mechanic, BJ came to her rescue. The personalized license plate read "Classy", a gift from BJ. Next to her car sat a shiny candy apple red SUV. That plate said, "Sassy".

"What? I can't believe it." She landed on her feet and circled her new wheels.

"Well, don't get too excited. It's not a new one but it will get you through a snowstorm. At least that's my hope." He'd overlapped his boots and leaned against the garage door.

"I don't care that it's not new. I love it." She approached and laid a hand on his chest. "But why'd you buy it? We can't afford any more expenses right now."

He caressed the palm of her hand with his thumb. "That last snowstorm. You scared the hell out of me. I don't know what I'd do if anything ever happened to you." Her heart skipped a beat when he stroked her wrist. "I know you won't listen to me when I tell you not to drive in bad weather, but it would give me peace of mind to know you are driving something safer."

"BJ." Her eyes watered. "No one's ever done anything like this for me before."

"Well, get used to it, hot stuff." He brushed away the tear that fell along her cheek. BJ's strong hands embraced her face. "No tears. So what do you say we give this thing a test drive and check out the shocks?" He led her past the front door and pressed her up against the back. His warm fingers slid under the blanket she wore, the only thing she was wearing. Her back curved and he crushed her to his chest.

"Thank you," she whispered. "Your love is the best gift I could ever receive." Her heart soared. "Merry Christmas, Mr. Spencer."

"Merry Christmas, future Mrs. Spencer." He held her close.

"You know, we never talked about whether or not I was going to change my name. I've had the same one for a long time, I'm kind of used to it," she joked.

BJ opened the back door of her Christmas present. Jessie stood and studied her future husband. "You know we could always bet on it. Another contest, so to speak." She winked.

BJ climbed in and patted the seat. "No thanks. Now get up here and sit on Santa's lap before I spank you for being a bad girl."

She didn't move. They both sounded good. Which one to choose?

"What are you waiting for?" He held out a hand to her.

"I can't decide." She pretended to weigh each option.

BJ's robe fell open, his thick dick stood at attention.

"I'll be right there, Santa." She adored her new gift but what it held inside was her most precious gift of all. The man she loved with all her heart.

THE END

OTHER BOOKS BY GINGER RING

Please check out these other great books available at fine online bookstores everywhere.

LOVE IS A DANGEROUS THING SERIES
The Gangster's Kiss
The Gangster's Woman
The Gangster's Hand

GENOA MAFIA SERIES
Madison's Mobster
Crossing Roman
Escaping Ryan
Taken to the Cleaner
Destroying Dominic
Playing Jasper
Chasing Arlo

STAND ALONE TITLES
The Pink Rose of the Prairie
Red Roses, Black Orchids

About the Authors

Ginger Ring is an award-winning author with a weakness for cheese, dark chocolate, and the Green Bay Packers. She loves reading, watching great movies, and has a quirky sense of humor. Publishing a book has been a lifelong dream of hers and she is excited to share her romantic stories with you. Her heroines are classy, sassy and in search of love and adventure. When Ginger isn't tracking down old gangster haunts or stopping at historical landmarks, you can find her on the backwaters of the Mississippi River fishing with her husband.

Find Ginger Ring at:
Website: *www.gingerring.com*
Facebook: *http://on.fb.me/IAGfuI*

Rarely will you find Ryan O'Leary in a state of rest; if he's not on the ice or kicking around a soccer ball, he's plotting his next story or out on the town with friends. His fun and flirty nature makes it possible for him to write the kind of romance that makes the reader both smile and tingle.

Find Ryan O'Leary at:
Facebook: *http://on.fb.me/1ajrxOL*